CHILLED TO THE CONE

KATHLEEN SUZETTE

Copyright © 2024 by Kathleen Suzette. All rights reserved. This book is a work of fiction. All names, characters, places and incidents are either products of the author's imagination, or used fictitiously. Any resemblance to actual events, locales or persons, living or dead, is entirely coincidental. All rights reserved. No part of this book may be reproduced or transmitted in any form or by any means, electronically or mechanical, without permission in writing from the author or publisher.

❦ Created with Vellum

SIGN UP

Sign up to receive my newsletter for updates on new releases and sales:

https://www.subscribepage.com/kathleen-suzette

Follow me on Facebook:

https://www.facebook.com/Kathleen-Suzette-Kate-Bell-authors-759206390932120

CHAPTER 1

"addie," a voice called. "Maddie."
"Huh?" I whispered groggily.
"Get up or you'll be late for school."
Mom.

The smell of pancakes woke me, and I was smiling before opening my eyes. Was I still dreaming? And what was that? I sniffed the air. Bacon? If there were pancakes and bacon, there had to be a tall glass of orange juice, too. And maybe even some scrambled eggs. My stomach growled at the thought. I blindly reached for my cat, Oliver, but his spot on the bed where he normally slept was empty. I opened my eyes to look for him, but he was nowhere to be seen. And then I remembered. The smell of bacon and pancakes wasn't a dream. My parents were here visiting for the week. I grinned and jumped out of bed, dressing quickly, and then pulling my black hair back in a low ponytail. Today was going to be a great day.

I brushed my teeth while looking in the mirror, and decided to skip the makeup. Although it was nearly impossible for my over-the-top pale skin to tan, I still managed to get a little color when I had laid out on the beach with my best friend, Chloe, the previous day. I didn't need the makeup today.

"Oh, my gosh, Mom, you didn't have to do all this," I said, coming up behind her where she stood flipping pancakes at the stove and wrapping my arms around her.

She chuckled and patted my hand where it was wrapped around her waist. "I know I didn't have to, but I wanted to. I never get to cook for you anymore, so I decided I better do as much cooking for you this week as I can."

I gave her a quick squeeze and released her. "Well, I'm certainly not going to complain about it then. I am the luckiest girl in the world."

Mom laughed and shook her head. "You're being silly now."

"I'm not being silly," I said, heading to the refrigerator. "Do we have orange juice? Oh, wait a minute, I bought some orange juice." I opened the refrigerator door and peered inside. "I'm surprised you were able to dig up enough ingredients to make breakfast with." I rarely had much in my refrigerator and cupboards, but I had gone shopping a week and a half ago. This was as stocked up as I got.

"I can make a fabulous spread out of nothing," Mom said. "And you had everything I needed."

"Good morning, Punkin," Dad said, carrying the morning newspaper to the table. "Did you sleep well?"

I nodded. "I slept great. But I always sleep great when you guys are visiting." There was a sudden tug at my heart. I missed my parents. They had moved to Arizona, along with my sister, to take care of both of my grandmothers. I was living in their house here in Lilac Bay, taking care of it while they were there. Everything in the house reminded me of them. I sighed, wishing they visited more often.

"What's that sigh for?" Dad asked, looking over the top of his glasses as he sat down at the table.

I shook my head. "Nothing. I just wish you both were able to visit more often. And I wish Hailey, and

Grandma Pearl and Grandma Ellen could also visit more often." I missed my family.

He nodded as he folded the newspaper and laid it on the table in front of himself. "I hear you. I wish we could come and visit more often, too. But you could also come to Arizona and visit us, too." One eyebrow rose.

"I know. And I will, I promise. Bill down at the bait and tackle shop said he wanted to go fishing with you when you came for a visit." I went to the cupboard and got out three large glasses, and brought them to the table. Some people may have opted for those tiny juice glasses when drinking orange juice, but not us. We loved orange juice, and we were not shy about using the big glasses.

Dad nodded. "I intend to take some time and hang out with Bill. I miss my old fishing buddy."

I smiled. Bill Washington was one of the nicest people around, and I knew they both missed one another.

"Breakfast is ready," Mom said as she brought a platter of bacon and scrambled eggs, and one with pancakes to the table. The syrup and butter were already there, and I sat at my usual place at the table.

"Aw, Mom, you went to too much effort. But it all

smells so good, and I'm glad you did." I inhaled slowly, taking it all in. This was the smell of home. I glanced at Oliver. He was chewing on something that looked suspiciously like bacon. He swallowed the last bit, licking his lips. His long orange and white fur had been recently brushed, and I knew my mother hadn't left out spoiling the newest member of the family.

Mom smiled as she handed me the platter of pancakes and handed the one with bacon and scrambled eggs to my dad. "That's what a mother is for. Do you have a busy day planned at work?"

I shook my head as I helped myself to two pancakes, putting them on my plate. "Just a regular day, but it's June, so that means it's probably going to be fairly busy."

"I'm glad the ice cream shop is thriving," Dad said. "It is thriving, isn't it?"

I nodded as I put butter on the hot pancakes. "Things have been good at the ice cream shop. I'm really glad because Cookie deserves it."

Mom passed me the plate of bacon and eggs, and I put three slices on my plate, along with a generous helping of scrambled eggs. Before digging in, I looked at my parents as they served themselves breakfast.

My throat tightened as I thought again about how much I missed them.

* * *

I parked in the small parking lot at the side of the ice cream shop and got out of my car just as Chloe pulled up. She parked and hurried out of her car, Brittany, an old Dodge that had seen better days but was nonetheless still running. "Oh man, I almost overslept. Mom is already here and probably has three flavors of ice cream made already."

I chuckled. "I know how your mom is. She probably has four made. We better get inside and help her out."

Chloe's mom, Cookie, owned Cookie's Creamery, the best ice cream store for miles around. Here in Lilac Bay, there were all sorts of homey seaside shops, and tourists came from miles around to visit each summer. But my favorite shop would always be Cookie's Creamery. Chloe and I have been best friends since we were little girls, and Cookie was a second mom to me. When I lost my job last year, she immediately offered me one at the ice cream shop. As a teenager I had worked my summers here, so it was like coming home again.

Chloe unlocked the door to the shop and let us in, locking it behind us. The lights were off in the shop's front, with a mellow glow of light coming from the open kitchen doorway. The shop wouldn't be open for nearly two more hours, and that would give us time to make the ice cream and cookies.

Chloe turned to say something to me when a scream rang through the shop. We stared at each other; our eyes wide. The first thing that sprang to mind was the fact that two nearby shops had been robbed in as many weeks. We ran to the kitchen.

CHAPTER 2

*C*ookie was standing at the entrance to the walk-in freezer with the door open, staring inside, when we rushed through the kitchen doorway.

"Mom!" Chloe shouted.

"What's wrong?" I said breathlessly.

She turned to look at us. Her face was deathly pale and her eyes wide. "I—I... Oh, no," she stammered, pressing a hand to her chest. "Oh, my."

"What is it?" I asked.

She shook her head. "There's a—oh, I don't even want to say it." She was on the verge of tears now, and when she breathed in, a low whistling sound was barely audible.

I sprinted over to the walk-in freezer, and that was when I saw what she was so upset about. I shook my head. "Oh, no." Lying on the floor, huddled in the freezer's corner, was a man. He was blue, with his eyes half-closed. "Oh, no."

"What?" Chloe said, crowding in behind me. When she saw the man, she gasped. "Oh, my gosh. Oh, no."

We all stood there in silence for what felt like an eternity, although in reality, it was probably only a few seconds.

"I'm calling Noah," I said, forcing myself to turn away. I dug through my purse, stepping back away from the freezer. "Don't touch anything."

"I don't understand," Cookie said, shaking her head. "How did he get in there? What happened? I don't understand."

I shook my head and dialed my boyfriend, Detective Noah Grayson. He answered on the second ring. "Hello?"

I swallowed before saying anything. "Noah, I need you down here at the ice cream shop right now. Please."

"Maddie, what's going on? What's wrong?"

I took a deep breath. "There's a guy here. We need you."

"A guy? What's going on? What's he doing?" I could hear the concern in his voice, and I realized I was probably confusing him.

"No, he's not doing anything. He's, well, he's in the freezer."

There was a pause. "What do you mean, he's in the freezer?"

I swallowed; my mouth had gone dry. "Chloe and I just got here, and Cookie opened the walk-in freezer, and there's a guy in there. He's dead, Noah."

There was another pause, and then, "I'll be right there. Don't touch anything."

I shook my head, even though he couldn't see me. "We won't." He hung up, and I stuck my phone in my pocket and turned back to Chloe and Cookie. Cookie looked like she was about to faint, and I hurried over with a kitchen stool for her. "Cookie, sit down. I don't want you to fall."

She did as I asked, shaking her head. "I don't understand this. Where did he come from? Why is he in my freezer?" She looked up at me, her eyes stricken. "Oh, my gosh. Do you think he could have gotten in there last night when we closed? Did we lock a man in the freezer?" Her face was red now as she spoke.

I shook my head. "No, we put ice cream away in there last night, and there was no one there then."

"We looked through the entire shop after we locked up last night," Chloe reminded her. "There's no way a man was hanging out in here and we didn't see him go into that freezer. There's just no way." She looked at me helplessly. "Right, Maddie? There's just no way something like that could happen."

I shook my head again. I needed to be strong for both of them. They had never come across a murder victim before, and this was distressing for them. Not that it wasn't distressing for me, because it was. I had seen some murder victims over the past year, and it was still upsetting for me, too.

"No, there's no way that could have happened. I'm absolutely sure of it." I took a deep breath. Noah would sort this out when he got here. Thank goodness for Noah.

Cookie looked up at me. "Then how could it have happened? How did he get into my freezer?"

I glanced at the open freezer door. I could just see the man's shoulder and part of his side from where I stood. How *did* he end up in our freezer? This was beyond worrying. Logically, I knew there was no way the man could have hidden in the shop and gotten into the freezer, but nagging at the back of my mind was a tiny hint of doubt that we had done something to contribute to what had happened to this man.

I shook my head. "I don't know." I licked my dry lips, went to the refrigerator, and grabbed a bottle of water. "Water?" I asked, looking over my shoulder.

They both nodded, and I grabbed two more bottles of water and brought them over to them. "I don't know what happened, but I know we are not responsible for what happened to that man."

I unscrewed the lid from my water bottle and took a big gulp. That was one thing I was certain of. We had nothing to do with this man's death. I just wished we knew how and why he had ended up dead here.

CHAPTER 3

While Noah and several other officers investigated what had happened to the man in our freezer, the three of us sat at a table in the front of the shop. It was nearly time to open, but I had a feeling that would not be happening today.

Cookie looked at her watch. "I haven't made any ice cream or cookies." She looked up at Chloe and me. "I suppose there's plenty of ice cream left over in the freezer." Her eyes widened as she realized what she had said. She shuddered. "Oh, goodness. The freezer."

I reached out and put a hand on hers. "Cookie, let's not worry about ice cream and cookies. We may not be able to open the shop today. In fact, I bet we won't."

She stared at me for a moment. "Do you think we won't? Is that a silly thing to ask? I mean, I realize there's a dead man in my freezer, but do you think we won't be able to open today?"

"Mom, I don't think we need to worry about it. Noah will let us know whether we can, but I think it would be best if we kept the shop closed. It's been a stressful day." Chloe took a sip of her water.

Cookie sighed. "I suppose you're right. It's not like I would have my mind on business anyway."

I nodded and patted her hand. "I don't think any of us could concentrate on our jobs today."

She took a sip of water from what was her second bottle. "I would just like to know what that man was doing in our freezer. It doesn't make sense, does it?"

Chloe and I shook our heads. "I don't understand why he didn't get out of the freezer," Chloe said, crossing her arms in front of herself. "There's a handle in there that you can use to open the door with."

"That's an excellent question," I agreed. "That's exactly what that handle is there for, and yet he didn't use it." That was what had me worried. He should have been able to let himself out. Unless he was already dead when he was put in there.

CHILLED TO THE CONE

I got up and removed the coffee maker from a lower cabinet along the wall. Last Christmas, we sold coffee and cocoa to go along with the cookies for those who weren't interested in ice cream when it was cold. The coffee wasn't fancy, but it had been popular, nonetheless. "I think we need coffee."

"I could use some coffee," Chloe said, getting up from the table and coming over to help. She got the packets of sugar from beneath the cabinet, and I got to work making the coffee. "Oh, what are we going to use for cream? We can't go back into the kitchen, I don't think." She glanced at the open door where Noah and the other officers were looking for clues as to how the man had ended up in our freezer.

I glanced at the open door just as Noah walked out of the kitchen. "Hey Noah, can you get us some cream, please?"

He looked puzzled for a moment, then nodded and disappeared back into the kitchen. He returned a few moments later with a carton of heavy cream.

I smiled. "Thanks. We need some caffeine to calm our nerves."

He nodded. "Won't caffeine rev your nerves up?"

I shrugged. "I don't know, but I need caffeine."

He smiled and went to the table where Cookie

was still sitting. "How are you doing, Cookie?" He sat across from her.

She shook her head. "I don't think I even know how I'm doing, Noah. I just don't understand how that man got into the freezer. And why didn't he let himself out? There's a handle inside to keep people from getting locked in."

He nodded. "We were looking at that handle, and it appears it's been tampered with. Officer Stevens went inside, and when we closed the door, he couldn't get out."

Cookie gasped. "What? Are you certain? Because nobody here has tampered with that door. Nobody would. I don't understand what's going on here." She looked like she was about to cry.

My heart went out to Cookie. She was really struggling with this, not that I blamed her. I couldn't understand how that man had gotten into our freezer, and I sure didn't know who had tampered with the door so that if somebody were trapped inside, they couldn't get out.

He nodded. "It's something we're going to look into. We've taken fingerprints from the door and inside the kitchen. We'll need all three of you, and

CHILLED TO THE CONE

your other employees to give us your fingerprints so we can eliminate them from the ones we took."

I poured four cups of coffee into paper cups, and Chloe helped me carry them back to the table along with the cream and sugar.

"Maybe this will help calm our nerves," I said, as I sat next to Noah. "I just can't imagine who would tamper with the freezer door."

He nodded and opened a packet of sugar and dumped it into his cup of coffee. "Like I said, it's something we're going to investigate." He looked intently at Cookie. "There isn't anyone who works here that you might wonder if they would tamper with the door, is there?"

Cookie's eyes widened. "No, of course not. I trust my employees implicitly. You can't think that some here did it. Please tell me you don't think that."

"Do any of you know the man in the freezer?" he asked, not answering Cookie's question.

"To tell you the truth, I didn't get a good look at him," Chloe said. "We were all so upset about finding somebody in there."

"I didn't recognize him," Cookie said, staring at her cup of coffee. She hadn't added any sugar or cream to it yet. "Honestly, I didn't want to look at him once I realized he was dead."

"That's understandable," he said and turned to me. "What about you, Maddie? Did you recognize him?"

I shook my head. "No, I didn't look at him closely either. Like Chloe said, finding him in there was such a shock."

He nodded. "Well, then, we'll run his fingerprints and see what we come up with. I know this has been upsetting for all of you, but we'll get to the bottom of this as quickly as possible."

"Noah, did it look like a struggle occurred? I just can't imagine how he ended up in the freezer." I took a sip of my coffee and added another packet of sugar.

He was quiet for a moment, stirring cream into his cup of coffee. After he finished stirring, he looked up at us. "It looks like somebody broke in through the back door."

Cookie stared at him in disbelief. "What? I didn't even notice. Are you sure?"

He nodded. "Somebody kicked the back door in, but they pushed it closed when they left so that it wouldn't be obvious. We've taken fingerprints from that, too, but they were probably wearing gloves."

"Wait a minute," I said, trying to fit these two

things together. "Somebody broke into the ice cream shop, and somebody ended up dead in our freezer. Why? Do you think the dead guy is the one who broke in? I can't imagine what he would want in the freezer." None of these things made sense to me.

"Maybe he was being nosy and decided to look around in there, and when the door was shut, he couldn't get out," Chloe said, looking at me wide-eyed.

Noah shrugged and took a sip of his coffee. "I don't know yet. You don't have any cameras out back, Cookie, so I can't see what happened. I'll ask the shop across the alley if they have a camera. But I didn't see one, so unless it's hidden well, I don't believe they do."

Cookie sighed. "I never really thought I needed a camera in my shop. I suppose it's silly in this day and age, isn't it? I should have bought some, and I should have put one in the front and the back, especially with the recent break-ins."

He nodded. "The shops around here are used to things being quiet and safe, and a lot of them probably don't have cameras. I think it would be best if you invested in some. In the meantime, have you noticed anything missing? What about the cash in the cash register?"

"I make a deposit at the bank every night, so there's only about a hundred dollars kept in the cash register drawer, and it's broken down into change and small bills. Let me see if it's still there." She got to her feet and hurried over to the cash register, and typed her code in. When the drawer sprang open, she shook her head. "No, it all appears to be here." She closed the drawer and looked at Noah. "I just don't understand this. I never keep anything of real value here, other than my ingredients. And that would be difficult for anyone to load up on a truck and steal, or even to do anything with it once they stole it. I don't understand what interest anybody would have in breaking in here."

"Is the laptop in your office still there?" I asked, looking at Cookie. I hadn't even thought about it until now.

"Yes, it's still there," Noah said. "We looked through her office, and other than the desk being rifled through, I can't tell if anything is missing. Cookie, I'll need you to look through your office and tell me if you notice anything."

Cookie nodded and came back over and sat down, and we all four looked at one another in silence for a few moments. I took a sip of my coffee, thinking this over. I couldn't imagine why anyone would want to break into the ice cream shop. Unless they believed we kept a lot of money in here after closing. But if that was the case, wouldn't they have at least tried to get into the cash register?

CHAPTER 4

The knock on the door had me on my feet, scurrying across the living room. I had been waiting impatiently for Noah to drop by and tell me what he had discovered about the body in our freezer.

When I opened the door, he smiled at me, but he looked tired. "Hey," I said.

He nodded. "Hey, yourself."

I stepped forward and went up on tiptoes to kiss him. "Are you hungry? Mom made meatloaf, and there's plenty left over."

He smiled again. "I love meatloaf."

"Well, come on in then." I grabbed him by the hand, and we went into the living room.

"Hi, Noah," Dad said. "How's it going? Maddie told us what happened this morning." I had filled him and my mother in on everything that I knew, although it wasn't much.

"Hello, Noah," Mom said, smiling sympathetically. "You look tired. Are you hungry? I made dinner, and I can warm something up for you."

He smiled. "I don't want to be a bother."

She shook her head and got to her feet. "It's no bother. Do you like meatloaf? I don't like to brag, but my meatloaf is pretty tasty."

"It's the best," I assured him.

"I love meatloaf, and I bet yours is the best," he said.

"I'll get you something to drink," I said as we headed into the kitchen. Noah and Dad sat on one side of the kitchen table while Mom reheated meatloaf, mashed potatoes, and buttered corn for Noah. I got some glasses out and put them at each of the settings for us. "We've got lemonade or iced tea."

"Lemonade would be great," Noah said, and sat down. "Janet, I hate putting you to any trouble, but I sure appreciate this. When I work late like this, sometimes I don't have time to get anything to eat until late."

She nodded without looking at him. "It's no trouble at all, Noah. It'll just take me a minute."

After pouring the lemonade for everyone, I sat across from Noah. "So, do you know anything about the guy in the freezer yet?" I had been trying to imagine a scenario where someone ended up in the freezer, but they all fell short. It didn't make sense that the guy was in there.

Noah took a sip of lemonade, and leaned back in his chair. "He had identification tucked inside the pocket of his jeans. His name is Charley Dade."

I inhaled. "Really? I know Charley Dade. His brother used to be the janitor at the high school, and Charlie worked there during the summer, too. That's a shame. He seemed nice."

"Charlie Dade?" Dad's brow furrowed. "I believe I know his father. Hugh Dade. We used to work together about twenty years ago. That's a real shame. Hugh's a good guy, and I hate to hear that he lost his son. I wonder what he was doing in the freezer at the ice cream shop?"

"I remember Hugh," Mom said from near the stove.

Noah nodded. "I'd like to know what he was doing in that freezer, too. I went to talk to Hugh earlier today, and he was surprised to hear where we found Charlie."

"I can't imagine losing a child," Mom said, shaking her head. "It's every parent's worst nightmare. Poor thing. I hope he has plenty of support to get him through this." She brought a plate loaded with food and set it in front of Noah.

"Oh, Janet, this looks delicious and smells fantastic. Thank you so much." Noah picked up a fork, hesitating. "Am I going to be eating alone?"

I nodded. "We ate a couple of hours ago. But don't worry about us watching you eat; you just eat."

He nodded and cut into the meatloaf with the edge of his fork. "I was hoping his father could give me some insight into what his son was up to, but he had no idea how he could have ended up in that freezer." He stuck a bite of meatloaf into his mouth and nodded appreciatively. When he swallowed, he turned to my mom. "This is excellent, Janet. I swear, I don't get home cooking often, and I sure appreciate this."

She smiled. "You're welcome, Noah. I'll be cooking all week, so drop in anytime you want."

He cut into his meatloaf again. "I'm going to take

you up on that offer. If I can get away from work, that is."

She reached over and patted his hand. "That's okay if you can't make it at dinner time. I'll make you a plate and hold it for you."

"That means you're going to stop by every night, Noah," I said.

He nodded. "No problem. I look forward to it."

"You know, I just thought of something," Dad said. "I worked with Hugh twenty years ago, but I ran into him three or four years ago. We got to talking, and he happened to mention that he was disappointed in Charley. I just can't remember why he said he was disappointed." Dad took a sip of his lemonade, his brow furrowed, trying to remember what the reason had been.

"Oh? He said he was disappointed?" Noah asked.

He nodded. "Yes, I distinctly remember him saying 'disappointed,' but I don't recall what the reason was."

I turned to Noah. "Do you think Charlie was responsible for the break-ins around town?" I didn't know if the two things were related, but it seemed like they had to be.

He shrugged. "We took his prints and all the prints we lifted from the ice cream shop and sent them for processing. I'm hoping we can get some answers soon. Maybe we'll get some answers about the break-ins, too."

"Maddie said the handle on the inside of the freezer was broken. Isn't that odd?" Mom asked.

He nodded. "It is, especially since Cookie swears it had been in working order previously."

"It's not like we have a reason to test it out frequently," I said. "But Cookie is on top of things. If there's paperwork to be filed, she gets it done immediately. If something even hints at breaking down, she gets it looked at or replaced before it has the opportunity to break down. And if something does manage to break down with no warning, it's replaced immediately. If there had been even a suggestion that something was wrong with that door, believe me, it would have been repaired or replaced right away."

Noah nodded and swallowed the food in his mouth before speaking. "I don't doubt that. I know Cookie well enough to know there's no way she would have let something like that slip through the cracks."

"Do you think Charley did something to the freezer door?" Dad asked. "Jimmied it for some reason?"

"I'm leaning in that direction, but since I don't have any idea why he would do it, I really don't know if he did. Nothing makes sense yet, but I'm sure as we look further into this, it will come together." He took a bite of his mashed potatoes and nodded. "These are not boxed mashed potatoes," he said after he had swallowed.

Mom chuckled. "No, those aren't boxed mashed potatoes. I prefer making them from fresh potatoes. There's just something about fresh mashed potatoes that the boxed kind cannot imitate."

"You're telling me," he agreed. "This is the best dinner I have had in some time."

Mom smiled. "I'm so happy to hear that."

I would have been offended that he didn't think a meal I had made was the best, but it had been a while since I had made dinner for him, and my mother's cooking really was that good. I made a mental note to make dinner for him again soon.

We sat and discussed what little we knew about Charlie Dade being found dead in the freezer at Cookie's Creamery while Noah finished his dinner. Nothing made sense at this point but, like Noah said, as we looked further into it, we would figure out how Charlie Dade ended up inside of it.

CHAPTER 5

"Cookie, she is as good as new." Art Stark stuck an electric screwdriver into the bag of tools he carried. "It won't give you any more trouble."

Cookie smiled. "Art, I can't tell you how happy that makes me. One of my biggest fears has always been that somebody might get stuck in that freezer, even though it had that handle on the inside. I still can't get over the fact that somebody did something to it so that it wouldn't work."

I glanced at Cookie as I stirred chocolate chips into the ice cream I was making. I hadn't realized she had worried about that door. Her worst nightmare really had come true.

Art nodded somberly. "Yes, I can see where that would be a concern, but if somebody hadn't tampered with it, that handle would have opened that door easily. I'm sorry for the trouble you've all experienced here." He glanced at me and Chloe, including us in the comment.

"I appreciate that," Cookie said, nodding. "I feel so terrible for that man and his family, though. What an awful thing to find out about your loved one."

He picked up his tool caddy. "Yeah, I can't imagine losing a child like that. I know Hugh Dade, and I know this is going to devastate him for the rest of his life." He sighed. "Well, if there isn't anything else that you need help with, I guess I better get going. I've got another job that I've got to get to work on."

Cookie nodded. "I appreciate it, Art. How much do I owe you?"

He put his baseball cap on his head. "I'll send you the bill. You can pay whenever you get around to it."

Cookie smiled. "Art, you are one of a kind. I'll get the payment to you immediately."

He smiled. "I knew you would. Well, you ladies have a good morning, and like I said, if anything else comes up, just call me, and I'll be right here to help you out."

"I appreciate it," Cookie said again as she walked him to the door to let him out. We weren't open yet, and we were still trying to get the day's cookies and ice cream made.

I turned to Chloe. "I still can't get over the fact that somebody did something to that door."

She nodded. "Me either. I'd like to know who did it and why."

The ice cream maker shifted into high gear as the chocolate chip ice cream thickened. I glanced at the back door. "I wonder how many businesses have been broken into."

"I know of at least four," she said as she shut off her ice cream machine. She got a bucket, set it on the counter, and then took the inside canister from the ice cream machine to pour it into the bucket. She was working on Cherries Jubilee, a tasty ice cream made with maraschino cherries, almonds, and crunchy bits of cobbler crust. It was one of my favorites.

"Four?" I asked. "I only heard about two. Noah didn't mention the other two to me."

"He probably just forgot," she said as she got a ladle, and began scooping the ice cream into the tub. It was thick but not frozen as hard as it would be when we scooped it. "It gives me the creeps, knowing somebody broke into our shop to rob us. They did something worse, of course, if Charlie Dade was the victim of murder, but it's scary that somebody is going around robbing businesses."

"It is scary, and I don't like it one bit." I glanced at the clock as Cookie returned from letting Art out the door.

"Well, girls, what else do we need to make?" Cookie put her hands on her hips and glanced around the kitchen.

"Oatmeal raisin cookies," I supplied. "Other than that, we're just about done."

She nodded and went to get the oats from the pantry. "I'll get that taken care of."

"It's just about time to open the shop. I'll go out front and wait on customers," I volunteered.

Chloe nodded as she finished transferring the ice cream to the tub.

I headed out front to unlock the door and then went back behind the counter. It wasn't two minutes later when the bell above the door jingled, and Deborah Carr, owner of one of the local gift shops, walked through the door. She smiled at me and hurried up to the counter. "Maddie, is it true? Was somebody murdered here yesterday?"

I hesitated. I knew that news traveled quickly in this town, but I was surprised this piece of information was out already. "To be honest, we don't really know what happened yet. Noah is working on the case, and I'm sure he will get it sorted out."

She nodded, placing both hands on the front counter. "I swear, I don't know what has gotten into the people of this town. All these robberies, and now a murder? It's awful."

I nodded. "It is. I hate hearing about all of it."

She glanced into the freezer with the ice cream. "Can I get a scoop of chocolate ice cream in a paper cup?"

"You bet," I said, grabbing an ice cream scoop. "What kind of toppings would you like?"

She shook her head. "No toppings. I like plain chocolate ice cream." She laughed. "My husband says I'm unimaginative, but I prefer to call myself loyal."

I chuckled. "I like that. When people criticize my choice of vanilla ice cream, I'm going to use that."

She grinned. "Maddie, do you have any idea who has been breaking into the businesses?"

I shook my head. "No. And if Noah does, he hasn't told me." I figured I had better cut her off from that line of questioning before it got started.

She leaned forward. "Well, the day before yesterday, I went to take the trash out to the dumpster in the alley, and when I was headed back inside, I noticed marks around the back door as if somebody had tried to pry it open." She shuddered. "I hate to think what could have happen had they gotten inside."

I hesitated with the ice cream scoop poised above the cup. "Really? Did you call the police?"

She shook her head. "No, because they didn't get inside. But I went to check my security cameras afterward, and there were two men dressed in black hoodies. They kept their heads down, so the cameras couldn't get a picture of their faces. But since someone was murdered, I'm thinking differently about it. I'm going to call Noah about it today."

I nodded. "Yes, you need to let him know. He needs to see the video. Even if they're not showing their faces, they might be familiar to him."

She crossed her arms in front of herself. "I'll definitely call him today. Like I said, I don't know what's gotten into this town, but the thieves need to be taken off the streets."

The thieves and the killers, I thought. I agreed with her. Something needed to be done.

CHAPTER 6

It had been three days since we found a dead man in our freezer, and I didn't have to go to work until later in the afternoon while Chloe was working the opening shift. With what little we knew about the victim, I wanted to spend any free time I had trying to gather information. My dad knew Charlie Dade's father, and I thought now was a great time to see what we could find out.

"I sure hate that Hugh Dade lost his son that way," Dad said with a sigh as I parked my car in front of Hugh's house.

I nodded. "I can't imagine how difficult it must be to lose a child. Really, to lose any family member is just awful. And since it was most likely murder, it makes it that much harder."

He turned to me. "I agree, murder makes it so much worse. But, losing a loved one under any circumstances is hard."

The only family members I had lost were my grandfathers. My father's father died when I was two, and my mother's father died six months after I was born. I didn't remember either of these men, and I felt the loss differently than either of my parents did. I knew I was fortunate to still have my remaining family members.

We got out of the car and headed to the front door. My dad knocked, and within a few moments, the door opened. Hugh Dade stood there looking forlorn, and as if he had gotten little sleep these past few days. I didn't blame him.

"Hello, Hugh," my dad said. "We heard about Charlie, and we wanted to stop by and tell you how sorry we are for your loss."

Hugh brightened a bit when he realized who it was that had knocked on his door. "Hi, Hank. I sure do appreciate you stopping by. I didn't know you were back in town. Did you move back?"

Dad shook his head. "No, Janet and I are just

visiting for the week. It's nice to get out of the Arizona heat for a bit and enjoy the cooler weather. Janet is meeting friends for brunch later, or I would have brought her by. You remember my daughter, Maddie, don't you?"

He smiled and nodded. "Yes, I remember Maddie. But I think you were still a teenager last time I saw you."

I smiled. "Hi, Hugh, I'm so sorry for your loss." Now that I had seen Hugh's face, I did remember him, but it had probably been ten years since I had seen him.

He nodded again. "I appreciate that. Would the two of you like to come in?"

"That would be nice," I said, as he pushed open the security door. We followed him into the living room and sat across from him on the couch.

"I still can't understand how Charlie ended up in the freezer at the ice cream shop. It doesn't make sense to me." He sighed, staring down at his hands.

"I work at Cookie's Creamery," I said, wanting him to know that I wasn't trying to keep anything from him should he discover it later.

His eyebrows shot up in surprise. "Oh? Were you there when he was found?"

I hesitated, then I nodded. "Yes, I was helping to open up the shop that morning."

He shook his head sympathetically. "I'm sorry you had to see that, then. It must have been shocking, to say the least."

I folded my hands in my lap. "It was quite the surprise. I don't think anything could have prepared us for finding him like that."

He was quiet for a moment, then he nodded. "Yes, I'm sure. When you found him, was there anything unusual that you saw? I don't know what it would be, but I just can't get over the fact that he was found there. Had anything else been messed with at the shop?"

I hesitated before answering. I didn't know how much Noah would want me to say. "It was just a regular morning at the ice cream shop. There wasn't anything out of the ordinary, if you want to know the truth. Have the police filled you in on everything they know?"

He nodded. "Oh, sure. They've told me plenty, but nothing that's of any use to help me understand why my son died in that freezer. It had to be a horrible death, and I'll never get the image out of my head. It's an image my mind has created, but there's no way to keep from doing that, you know. He was my firstborn child, and I never once considered that he might die before me." Hugh looked like he was on the verge of tears, and my heart went out to him.

"I couldn't have imagined it either," Dad said. "One never expects their child to die first. I'm so sorry you're going through this."

Hugh rubbed his eyes and sighed. "No, I never imagined it. Never. Maddie, are you dating that detective at the police station?"

I nodded. "Yes, I'm dating Noah Grayson."

"I heard that, but I wasn't sure." He looked at an upright piano against the wall that had family pictures on it. "I always had high hopes for my sons. They were both so smart when they were small, but I have to admit that I've been disappointed by them. They both dropped out of college, and they both tend to job-hop. I don't know why they can't hold onto a job for more than a year or two. Both of them are smart. Very smart. But it's like they don't even put out any effort." He frowned. "Ryan opened a bicycle rental shop at the beach. Says he intends to bring in other things that could be rented, too, like kites and surfboards. Seems like a flimsy business, but maybe he'll stick with it." He snorted. "A bicycle rental shop."

"Sometimes it's hard to get your footing in life," I said. I had done enough of my own struggling after losing my job last year. "The bicycle rental business sounds interesting. Hopefully he will have a lot of success with it."

His eyes met mine. "I suppose it can take a while. But it doesn't make sense. I thought they would both be married and have kids by now. Charlie was seeing Charlene Douglas. Charlie and Charlie, we called them." He smiled at the memory. "I thought for a while they would get married, but then they broke up. Charlie said he didn't want to settle down and have kids, and that shocked me. He was thirty-five, you know. He should have had a couple of little ones by now. But then, a woman named Ashley Myers came back into his life about two months ago. They had dated before Charlene came around. He said he and Ashley were seeing each other again, and that surprised me because when they broke up, he was adamant that he didn't want anything to do with her."

"Ashley Myers?" I said. "Does she work at the nail salon near the highway?"

He shrugged. "I'm not sure, to be honest. But it seems like the two of them had an up-and-down relationship. I didn't like her as well as I did Charlene."

"Sometimes it takes time for kids to get settled in with whoever they've chosen to spend their life with," Dad said.

He looked up at him. "Yeah, I guess so. Maybe if somebody hadn't killed Charlie, they would have gotten married and had kids. Charlene was better for him, though. She was more the motherly type. Ashley wouldn't have made a good mother. She's too self-absorbed."

"I think I know Ashley. She's a few years younger than Charlie, right?" I asked. I knew Charlene as well, and made a mental note to talk to her.

He nodded. "Yeah, five or six years younger, I think."

I felt sorry for Hugh. He seemed to want the best for his kids but couldn't understand the paths they had taken in life. We stayed and talked to him for a few more minutes, but he kept repeating that he had no idea what had happened to his son. I had hoped we would get some kind of information that would help us understand who had killed his son.

CHAPTER 7

"How is your mom doing?" I asked Chloe as I took a sip of frozen lemonade. We were off work today and we were taking a stroll along the beach to see if we could find out anything about Charlie Dade's death.

She sighed, looking off at the water. "She's still really upset about everything. I feel so bad for her, and I wish I could do something to make her feel better."

I nodded as we walked, the sand tugging at my flip-flops. "I really hate that she's so upset by this. I don't blame her, of course, that was an awful thing to see. But I feel like she kind of blames herself for some reason, and I don't understand why." I hadn't gotten to see Cookie the previous day when I went to work. She had left early, saying she hadn't felt well.

Chloe took a sip of her frozen raspberry lemonade. "Yeah, I kind of think she does. I talked to her about it yesterday, but there's no reasoning with her."

I sighed. "There's no way she should blame herself. She couldn't have known someone was going to break into the shop that night, and the freezer door was in good working order as far as she knew. Someone sabotaged it so that it wouldn't unlock." That was the thing that really bothered me. Who would have done it? Did the killer break into the shop with Charlie? Or could it have been one of the other employees at the shop? Cookie only employed part-time employees other than Chloe and me, most of whom were high school kids or were a few years younger than us. Nobody who worked seemed like they would have done something like that. And if they had, who would it have been?

"I know, and I told her the same thing. I think she's just going to need a little time to step back and look at things objectively. Whoever killed Charlie had to have known he was going to break into the ice cream shop. But why would he go into the freezer, and how would the killer know he would? I don't think anybody from the shop could have done it." She turned to look at me imploring me to agree with her.

I nodded. "I don't think they would either." We had discussed the possibility of somebody at the shop having sabotaged the freezer door, but nobody was suspicious enough to warrant a closer look. Noah had agreed with us.

Hugh Dade had mentioned that his son Ryan had opened a bicycle rental business near the beach, and we were on our way to see if we could get any information from him. The shop sat near the edge of the beach where some other shops were located that sold beachwear, surfboards, and there was a snack shop.

As we approached the bike rental shop, I could see two-seater bikes, as well as single bikes parked out front with orange flags on them to alert vehicles of their presence while being ridden.

We stepped inside the tiny, cool shop as Ryan waited on a customer. They finished paying for their bike rental, and he handed them a key.

He smiled when he saw us. "Good morning, ladies. I haven't seen you two around for a while. How can I help you?"

I smiled back. "I really love those two-seater bikes you have out front."

Ryan had long, curly blond hair and a deep tan. He had the typical look of a surfer guy.

He nodded. "Yeah, those are popular. If you come by on the weekend, you'd better do it early, or else you won't be able to get one. They rent for twenty-five dollars an hour. Are you interested?"

"I would love to go for a ride on the beach. It's so calming," Chloe said. "But we were just stopping in to see how much it costs. Maddie's parents are in town, and we're trying to figure out what we're going to do this weekend."

He leaned on the counter. "Well, you'd better put in a reservation if that's what you decide to do. Like I said, they'll all be gone otherwise."

I nodded. "Ryan, we're sorry to hear about your brother."

He frowned and glanced at Chloe. "I hope you two didn't find him that morning."

I hesitated before nodding and saying, "Yes, we found him."

He dropped his head and shook it, then looked up at us again. "I'm sorry to hear that." He drew in a deep breath. "I just hope the police figure out who killed him and that they do it quickly. I can't stand sitting around knowing that a killer is on the loose. Feels like my hands are tied, and that's a frustrating feeling."

"We feel the same way," Chloe said. She leaned on our side of the counter. "Do you have any idea who might have wanted to hurt him?"

He bit his bottom lip for a moment. "Well, I can't swear to anything, but if I were going to take a wild guess, then I would guess it had to be Charlie's girlfriend. Ashley Myers."

"Why would you say that?" I asked.

He shrugged. "Because the two of them couldn't stand each other. I know what you're thinking, why were they dating if they couldn't stand each other, right? Believe me, I've asked myself that too many times to count, and I asked him that too. I don't think he even knew why he was with her, to be honest, and they broke up a few times over the past several years. He even dated Charlene Douglas for a while, but he went back to Ashley. It was like they were magnet and steel. They couldn't stay apart for very long."

"Really?" I asked. "They broke up a bunch of times?"

He nodded. "A bunch. I don't know what he saw in her. Sure, she was cute, but it was like all she wanted to do was fight with him. She was always calling him, causing trouble for him, and always arguing with him. She was never happy. It didn't matter what he did for her; she complained about it. He should have stuck with Charlene."

"That doesn't sound like a healthy relationship to me," I said. "We talked to your dad yesterday, and I feel so bad for him. But he mentioned that the two of them had broken up but then got back together again."

He sighed. "Oh yeah, it happens all the time. My dad isn't even aware of how often it happens. Charlie tried to keep that kind of thing from him because it embarrassed him. I didn't want to stick my nose into things and tell our dad what was going on, so I didn't. But I saw her punch him in the chest a couple of times when she got angry with him."

I was shocked at this. "Really? She got physically violent with him?"

"Or was she just playing around?" Chloe asked.

He shook his head. "It didn't look like playing to me. I told Charlie there was no reason he should stay with her. Getting physically violent was crossing a line, and he ought to break up with her."

"That's awful. I wouldn't tolerate something like that," I said, crossing my arms in front of myself, taking this in. "Why would he keep going back to her if she was treating him that way?"

He shook his head. "I wish I knew. And I wish I had been more proactive in encouraging him to see somebody else and leave her alone. Charlene was perfect for him, and I should have encouraged him more to stay with her. Makes me feel a little responsible for him dying if Ashley is the one who killed him. And I wouldn't be one bit surprised if she was."

"Does she work at the nail shop down near the highway?" I asked.

He nodded. "Yeah, she's worked there for a few years, I think. I've been trying to stay away from there, but what I really want to do is confront her about murdering my brother."

I shook my head. "No, don't do that. Have you told Detective Grayson about this?"

He absently picked up a bolt from the counter. "No, I haven't told him yet. I don't even know why I didn't mention it to him, but I didn't. I think I'm going to stop by the police station and talk to him when I get off work tonight."

"I think you should definitely talk to him," I said. "He needs to know what was going on between Charlie and Ashley."

He nodded. "I'm going to do it then. I don't know why I've been putting it off. And if Ashley killed him, she's going to be sorry."

"If she killed him," Chloe said, "why would she have done it at the ice cream shop?"

He shrugged. "I guess I don't know. But I've heard about the recent break-ins. I think Ashley might be behind them. She and her brother, Rickey. Rickey has been to jail a few times. Maybe Charlie knew what they were up to, and he tried to stop her, and the two of them shoved him into that freezer. That's the only thing I can think of."

We stayed and talked to Ryan for a while before moving on. What he said about Ashley and her brother Rickey made me wonder if he was right about them killing Charlie.

CHAPTER 8

After I dropped Chloe off at her apartment, I drove to the police station to see what Noah was up to. The officer at the reception desk buzzed me through, and I knocked on his door while trying to balance two iced coffees. It was warmer today than the weatherman had expected, and iced coffees were in order. When Noah hollered for me to come in, I held both cups against myself while opening the door with my free hand.

His eyebrows raised when he saw me. "Well, to what do I owe the pleasure?"

I stepped inside and closed the door with my foot, then crossed the small room and placed his iced coffee on the desk in front of him. "I just thought I would stop in and see how my handsome boyfriend was doing with his latest case." I leaned over and kissed him and then sat in the chair in front of his desk. "So, how goes it?"

He shook his head and sighed. "Not nearly as well as I had hoped. What's up with you? What are you doing on your day off?"

I took a sip of my iced coffee. I hadn't seen much of him since he began investigating this case, and I needed to catch up with him. He had only managed to stop by my house for dinner one time so far. "Oh, you know, just wandering around and looking for people to talk to." I filled him in on what Hugh and Ryan Dade told me, and he looked at me with raised eyebrows.

"Wait, Ryan knew that Charlie's girlfriend had been physical with him, and he didn't mention it to me?"

I shrugged. "That's what he says."

He sighed in exasperation and took a long swig of his iced coffee. "This is tasty. Thanks for bringing it. I can't imagine why Ryan didn't tell me this earlier. It would have been good to know that kind of information."

I nodded. "But still, why did Charlie end up dead

in Cookie's walk-in freezer? Did Charlie, Ashley, and her brother Rickey all break in?" Noah had already told me that his death was definitely a murder.

"It's possible," he said, shaking his head. "I don't know."

I sighed. "The killer has to have messed up and left some clues somewhere. They just have to."

He sat back in his chair and took another sip of his iced coffee. "I got the report back from the medical examiner's office."

I was all ears. "What did it say?"

His eyes met mine. "Not as much as I had hoped. There were abrasions on the tips of his fingers that looked like they were made from trying to scratch at the door."

I groaned. "That's just sad." I could have done without that picture in my mind.

He nodded. "And there was a bruise on his ribs."

I looked at him. "A bruise? What kind of bruise? How big was it?"

"About the size that would be made if somebody punched him really hard. And it was dark colored, and he had most likely received it shortly before his death."

My eyes widened. "Ashley. It has to be her. She got

mad at him, punched him in the ribs, and then locked him in the freezer at the ice cream shop."

"Certainly a possibility. But it seems that it would have taken a bit of strength to disable the handle on the inside of the freezer door. I'm not sure if she would have had the strength to do that." He took another sip of his iced coffee, deep in thought.

"That's where her brother Rickey comes in. But more importantly, why would Charlie stand there and allow that? Say they all break in, they're looking for valuables, and Rickey goes into the freezer and uses some kind of weapon to disable the door handle from the inside. What is Charlie doing in the meantime?"

He looked at me. "Maybe they held a gun on him so he couldn't escape or fight back."

"Maybe. But we're not aware of a gun being used in any of the robberies so far. Right? Why bring one now? And why not shoot him if they had one? Why freeze him to death?" I took a sip of my iced coffee. There were still too many unanswered questions.

"Those are excellent questions, and I'm afraid I don't have any answers yet. But I'm going to find out."

"Did he have any drugs or alcohol in his system? Maybe he wasn't thinking clearly when they broke in, and he didn't realize what they were doing. And he had no idea he was about to die in that freezer." That was the only thing I could come up with at this point. Why would he willingly stand there and allow the killer to disable the handle? And how did they get him inside the freezer without him fighting back?

"No drugs or alcohol. And how did they get him inside that freezer?" he said, echoing my thoughts.

"Oh, look at that. You're a mind reader. That's the same question I just thought of." I grinned at him.

He chuckled and took another sip of his iced coffee. "I told you I was talented."

I laughed. "You did. But I did not know that mind reading was part of your talent. So, what do you think? Why would that happen?"

He gazed at me while he thought this over and finally shook his head. "I don't know yet."

"Okay, fair enough. We've got to get to the bottom of this. What else did he have on him? Were there any clues among his personal possessions?"

He sighed. "Didn't I tell you? There was a single key in the front pocket of his jeans."

I shook my head. "No, you didn't tell me that. Do we know what the key is for?"

"Nope. I don't know what it goes to yet. I showed it to his father, but he didn't recognize the key."

"What about his brother? Did you show it to him? Maybe he has some idea of what it might go to. It wasn't a car key, right?"

He shook his head. "No, not a car key. It looks more like it goes to a lock. Ryan said it looked like the kind of key that might go to a chain lock similar to what he used on the bicycles he rents out, but that Charlie hadn't borrowed any of his bikes."

"So, it could belong to almost anything." I took a long sip of my iced coffee as I thought about this. "Where did he work?"

"Over at the electronics store on Broadway."

"He sold electronics," I said. "I wonder if it went to something there at the electronics store. Maybe they keep something locked up that only the employees have access to. Like a clear Plexiglas cabinet full of merchandise? To keep customers from stealing something."

He nodded. "That's a good idea. It could be to protect laptops or gaming systems. Or maybe their break room is kept locked, so customers don't wander back there. Or even the bathroom. Some stores don't allow the public to use them."

I stretched and yawned. "I need to get to bed earlier at night. But you might be right about a break room or a restroom. That store isn't big, so they wouldn't want customers wandering around in the back with no one to watch them. It might not mean anything then. It's not like it was going to help them break into Cookie's shop."

He nodded. "Exactly. I'll keep looking. Oh, and there was a lot of sand in his shoes."

"That could mean anything since we live at the beach. Maybe they went for a moonlight stroll before breaking in."

He nodded. "Could have."

"You need to take me out to dinner. You've been neglecting me."

He smiled. "Haven't I? I was just thinking the same thing this morning. I've got a meeting with the chief this evening, but maybe we can go tomorrow."

I grinned. "See? There you go, reading my mind again. You really are talented."

He chuckled.

I needed to stop by the electronics store and see if I could figure out what that key might go to.

CHAPTER 9

"I could really use a new laptop, but I can't afford one," Chloe said as she parked Brittany in the small parking lot next to the electronics store.

I nodded. "Me too. I think I'm going to save up for a nice one, though, and just use my phone for as much as I can until I have the money for it." Although I would have loved to have gotten a new laptop now, I didn't want a cheap one that wouldn't last, and I wasn't going to put a more expensive one on my credit card. Patience was key here.

We got out of the car and headed to the shop. Once we stepped inside, I felt my resolve not to spend any money weakening. There were laptops and desktop computers set up on a long table in the middle of the shop. Lining the walls were shelves with an assortment of electronics, along with gaming systems I had no interest in. But walking into one of these places was enough to make any resolute person cave.

A woman waited on customers at the cash register, while a salesperson glanced in our direction as we went to check out the laptops on the table. I kept an eye on him as we looked over the machines.

"I want one so bad," I whispered to Chloe.

She nodded. "Me too. I'm not going to spend the money though, because I know it will just get me into trouble."

"Good afternoon, ladies," the salesman said, stepping up to the table. "Is there anything I can help you with?"

I smiled at him after glancing at the laptop on the table. "Jared? Jared Stone?" I was certain I had gone to school with him, but he looked different somehow.

He grinned. "Yeah, oh my gosh, what was I thinking? Maddie and Chloe," he chuckled. "I knew I knew you as soon as you walked through the door, but I don't know. I guess I've had my mind on other things lately, and it just completely slipped my mind that I already knew you." He laughed again, and his cheeks turned pink. "I don't know if that made any sense."

I smiled. "How have you been, Jared? You look good."

He stood taller. "Yeah, I lost sixty pounds a couple of years ago and I haven't felt this good since—well, I don't know, since I was born," he laughed. "How have you two been?"

"You look really good, Jared," Chloe said. "And I like the beard. It suits you."

He beamed. "Wow, you two are good for my ego. I might just have to give you guys a discount on your next laptop."

I laughed. Jared had been shy and awkward in school, but he had really blossomed. "Well then, I think you've gotten taller, too. Haven't you gotten taller? That should be good for an extra fifty bucks off, right?"

We all laughed. "Yeah, it just might be," he said. "Seriously though, how have you two been?"

I sighed. "We've been really good. Jared, did you hear about that murder last week? The one that happened at the ice cream shop?"

He nodded and glanced at Chloe. "I heard about it.

Chloe, did that happen at your mom's ice cream shop? Or the other one across town?"

Chloe nodded. "Yeah, it was at my mom's shop. It was a terrible surprise. My poor mom is really struggling to get past it."

His brow furrowed. "What happened? How did he end up in the freezer?"

She shrugged. "I wish we knew. Honestly, we don't have any idea what he was doing there, or how he ended up in the freezer. There's a handle on the inside of the freezer that prevents you from getting locked inside, but it looks like it was damaged somehow."

At that moment, I felt sorry for Chloe. I knew she wanted to say so much more because she didn't want people to think that her mom hadn't kept the walk-in freezer in working condition.

"Didn't the guy who was killed last week work here?" I asked, changing the subject.

He hesitated, a look of uncertainty crossing his face. "Yeah, Charlie worked here, all right. He was the lead salesman." He rolled his eyes. "We're not supposed to talk about it."

"You say lead salesman like it wasn't deserved?" I asked, hoping he would expand on his feelings about him.

He snorted and stepped closer. "Well, it's like this, Charlie was one of those people who could talk his way into or out of anything. He had no business being the lead salesperson, if you want my opinion. But like I said, he could talk his way into or out of anything. I was supposed to be up for that promotion, but he lied about me about some things, and our boss believed him. Got me put on probation." He shoved his hands into his pockets and jingled his keys.

"Oh, I'm so sorry," I said. "It's hard working with people like that." Jared's face flushed dark pink as he spoke.

He nodded. "He was an awful person. And an awful salesman. He thought he was the king of sales, but he was really just a jerk. We have customers coming in here all the time complaining about him, but for some reason, our boss thought he was fantastic and would ignore them."

"How could he ignore complaints about him?" Chloe asked. "If he does that often enough, it's going to hurt business."

He nodded soberly. "Yeah, that's what I said. But Charlie could do no wrong. We had a guy come in here a couple of weeks ago and accuse him of selling him a pre-owned laptop as if it were new. Charlie denied it, but the guy swore up and down that it was used, and he was angry because it failed on him. He tried to get his money back, but he had had it for a few months by that time, and it was too late. The thing is, it really was a pre-owned laptop, and he shouldn't have sold it to him for the price that he did."

I shook my head. "Why would your boss allow him to get away with something like that? Why didn't he make it right for the customer?"

He shrugged, but his face had turned red now. "Like I said, Charlie could do no wrong. That customer took it up with corporate, though, and our boss got into trouble, although he wouldn't tell us the details."

"It must have made you angry that he got your promotion," Chloe said.

He nodded. "Oh yeah, it made me angry, alright. I made far more sales than he ever did. I worked my tail off while he hung out and gossiped with our boss. Don't tell anybody, but I'm hunting for another job. I will not be treated that way. Not when I can find something better. I know my worth, and I am not going to hang around here after that." The muscle in his jaw twitched. "I'm not surprised Charlie was murdered. Maybe that's a terrible thing to say, but he was a real jerk. It wouldn't surprise me if he made the wrong person angry. I don't know why or how he could have ended up in the ice cream shop freezer though. That part is a little weird."

I nodded. "It is a little weird."

He breathed out. "It's a good thing someone killed him because I wasn't going to let him get away with stealing my promotion. I planned to take this up the corporate ladder and get him and my boss fired. I'm still going to do it. They don't know what a valuable employee they have in me."

Jared sounded bitter. Not that I blamed him. But was he bitter enough to commit murder?

We talked for a few more minutes, and then we left.

"He seemed very angry, didn't he?" Chloe asked as we got into the car.

"He certainly did." I didn't know if Jared was angry enough to kill Charlie, but I was going to find out.

CHAPTER 10

I placed a tub of pistachio ice cream into the freezer and looked up as the bell over the door jingled and my favorite customer, Estelle Smith, breezed in. She was wearing a floppy straw hat and had a cute floral canvas bag slung across her body.

"Good morning, Estelle," I said. "It's a beautiful day, isn't it?"

She nodded, grinning. "It is a wonderful day." She hurried up to the front counter and glanced into the freezer at the tubs of ice cream. "I stopped by yesterday and you weren't here. I hope everything was okay." She looked up at me.

I nodded, leaning on the counter. "Yes, I worked

CHILLED TO THE CONE

the late shift yesterday. Sorry I missed you. How have you been?" Estelle was a retired librarian from the county library. She was a confessed chocoholic, and she came in nearly every day for ice cream.

"Well, as long as everything is all right," she said and chuckled. "I think I'm going to get some of that Oreo Cookie Blast." She pointed through the glass at the tub of ice cream. "And how about some fudge sauce on top?"

I nodded. "You got it. Would you like a waffle cup?"

"Yes, that would be fine. Say, Maddie, I heard there was a murder here." She whispered the last part, glancing around the shop, but only two other customers were sitting at tables in the far corner. I nodded somberly. "Yes, I'm afraid somebody died in the freezer. Cookie is just beside herself about it."

She nodded. "I hate to hear that. I've heard about the break-ins at the local businesses, and I just don't know what this world is coming to." She shook her head. "I certainly hope Noah can find the murderer soon."

I grabbed my ice cream scoop and a waffle cone. "I know he's doing his best to do just that."

"You know, I was driving past the ice cream shop

65

late that night, and I saw three people in hooded sweatshirts, walking down the street. I don't know where they were headed, but I got a bad feeling about them. Maybe I should have reported them."

I stopped and turned to her. "Oh? The night the man was found dead? Or the night after?" I scooped a generous amount of the Oreo ice cream into the waffle cup.

She shook her head. "I believe it was the night that young man was murdered. I heard about it the next day, and they said it had happened that night. I should have mentioned it to Chloe when I was in here, but I had forgotten about it. It just suddenly came to me last night and I had to think hard about what night it was. But it was last Tuesday night because I had to run to the drugstore to get some allergy medicine. I don't usually go anywhere at night, but my allergies have been bothering me something terrible, and I didn't want to try to sleep without getting something to relieve it."

I hesitated. "Were they males or females? Could you tell how old they were? Were they teenagers?" This was interesting information, and I hoped that she could remember more.

She sighed. "Well, it was really hard to tell

because, like I said, they were wearing hooded sweatshirts, and their hoods were pulled up over their heads, and sort of covering part of their faces, like some of them do. If I had to guess, I would say there was one female and two males. But I didn't see where they were going. It could have just been some teens out for a stroll. I know they were young, but I can't swear they were teens, though."

I nodded as I poured fudge onto her ice cream. "Whipped cream? Cherry?"

She nodded. "Please."

I gave it a generous squirt of whipped cream and placed the cherry on top. "Cookie?"

"How about a chocolate chip?"

I went to get her a cookie when Chloe and Cookie came out from the back room, each carrying a bucket of ice.

Chloe smiled. "Good morning, Estelle."

"Good morning, Chloe. Good morning, Cookie." Estelle grinned at them. "It's a beautiful day."

Cookie smiled as I went to the cash register to ring up Estelle's ice cream order. "Good morning, Estelle," she said. "How are you doing?" She set the tub of ice cream she was carrying into the freezer and turned to her.

"I'm doing fine, Cookie," Estelle said. "I'm so sorry about what happened last week."

Cookie nodded soberly. "Thank you. I'm sure Noah will get things sorted out soon." She glanced at me.

"I'm sure he will," I agreed.

I rang up Estelle's ice cream, and after chatting a few more moments, she left. A moment later the bell over the door rang again as Charlene Douglas walked through it.

I smiled. "Hi, Charlene." Now was our chance to find out what she knew.

She smiled wanly as she approached the counter. Charlene was around 5'6" tall and thin, with shoulder length blonde hair. There were so many things that I wanted to ask her about her former boyfriend, Charlie Dade. "Hi Maddie." She nodded at Chloe and Cookie.

"Charlene, I'm so sorry about Charlie," I said.

"Charlene, I'm sorry too," Chloe said.

Cookie nodded. "I am, too."

Charlene took a deep breath. "Thanks. Charlie and I had broken up a while ago, but I wasn't over him. I miss him."

My heart went out to her. "It must be so hard. I can't imagine what you're going through."

Tears came to her eyes, and she blinked them away. "Charlie was a good guy. The only person I can think of who might want to hurt him was Ashley. I know that probably sounds crazy, but the two of them fought all the time. Charlie told me all about it when we were dating. That's why it was so devastating when he went back to her. Why would he want to go back to her if she was hurting him?"

I shook my head. "It must have been so hard when he told you he was going back to someone who had hurt him."

She closed her eyes and nodded. When she opened them, there were tears again. "It was crazy. I just couldn't understand it. I didn't stop by for ice cream—it's taken me this long to come in here because it just makes me sick thinking how he died here. But I wondered if any of you have any idea why he would have been here that night."

I shook my head. "No, we have no idea. I was hoping you might know."

She sighed. "I don't have any idea. It doesn't make any sense at all. I talked to your boyfriend the other day. I know he's working hard to find his killer, and I just hope it doesn't take long."

I nodded. "I know Noah will find his killer soon."

"There's no reason for him to have been here," Chloe said, grabbing a damp cloth and running it over the counter.

Charlene brushed a lock of hair off her forehead. "I haven't slept since I found out. I keep trying to come up with a reason he would have ended up here when he was killed. There has to be some explanation, but I can't think of one."

"I don't know either," Cookie spoke up. "As Chloe said, there was no reason for him to have been here."

I knew Cookie worried about how it looked for Charlie ending up in our freezer, but I didn't think that Charlene was blaming us in the least.

Charlene nodded and looked away. "I guess I knew I wouldn't find any answers here, but I had to come by anyway." She turned back to us. "I'm sorry it happened here. I'm sure it has been distressing for you all."

I nodded. "It has been."

She inhaled. "Well, I won't bother you any longer. I've got to get to work."

"I'm sorry for your loss, Charlene," Cookie said.

She smiled sadly and nodded. "Thanks." Then she turned and left the shop.

"Poor Charlene," Chloe said.

Cookie sighed tiredly. "I hate that the whole world knows that somebody died in my ice cream freezer."

I shook my head. "Nobody blames you, Cookie. You can't take responsibility for this."

She made a face. "I know, but I can't help it. I won't be able to sleep until that young man's killer is found."

Cookie looked as if she hadn't gotten a bit of sleep since we had discovered Charlie Dade in our freezer. My heart went out to her. I hated that she felt so badly about this, but I couldn't blame her either. We had to find the killer.

CHAPTER 11

Over the next two days, not much had changed with the case. Noah was frustrated, and I was sad that Charlie's killer had yet to be caught. My dad had plans to go fishing with Bill Washington, and Chloe and I had the day off, so we decided to spend the day laying out on the beach and trying to forget about the investigation. Emphasis on the word 'try' because the details of the case went through my mind constantly. Not to mention poor Chloe and Cookie. They were more worried about this than I was.

If you're going to lie out on the beach, you need a book, an umbrella, suntan lotion, and snacks and drinks. Lots of snacks and drinks. We had everything but the snacks and drinks, so we stopped by Bill's bait shop to pick up a few things. Dad and Bill had plans to go fishing while his wife, Henrietta, watched the shop. Mom had come along with us to visit with Henrietta.

When we got to the bait shop, we found the door was locked. We pulled on it twice, thinking it was just sticking, but it was firmly locked. I peered in through the window and saw Bill sweeping something up. I knocked on the window and when he realized it was us, he smiled and hurried over to the door to unlock it.

"Good morning, friends," he said, smiling. "What brings you by?"

"I thought we were going to go fishing, Bill," Dad said, his brow furrowed.

Bill squinted at my dad, then sighed. "Of course we were, Hank. I'm so sorry, I'm not myself today. But right now, I've got a little something to take care of."

I leaned to the right to see past Bill. His behavior was odd since it was well past his normal opening time, and he wasn't stepping back to let us in. Then I saw it.

"Bill, what happened?" Racks of chips and candy

were knocked over on the floor behind him. The place looked like a small tornado had whipped through.

His eyes widened. "I'm afraid the thief that's been breaking into businesses around town has hit my store."

"Oh no," Chloe said.

"That's terrible," Mom said.

Henrietta appeared from the tiny backroom carrying a large black plastic trash bag. Her eyes were red, but when she saw us, she smiled. "Well, good morning, folks." She glanced at the mess on the floor. "Maybe not such a good morning."

"Did you call the police?" Dad asked.

Bill shook his head and stepped back, allowing us into the store, then locked the door behind us. "No. I'll take care of this."

I was surprised that he hadn't called the police. "Bill, you need to call the police. They need to know about this."

He shook his head without looking at me. "I'll take care of it."

I looked helplessly at Henrietta. She blinked back tears, forcing herself to smile. "It will be all right," she assured us.

"Did they take anything?" I asked, turning to Bill. It didn't make sense not to call the police.

He nodded without looking at me. "Yes, they stole the entire cash register."

Chloe and I gasped. "The whole thing?" Chloe asked.

Bill went back to sweeping. The thieves had knocked over racks and stomped on bags of chips, and they were everywhere.

"Yes, I had a rather old cash register. I bought it back in the '90s, and since it was still working, I never got around to replacing it with a newer model. It was pretty small, so it probably wasn't any trouble for them to pick it up and run with it."

"That's terrible," Dad murmured.

"I'm so sorry," I said. "Let us help you clean up." I went over to one of the wire racks and set it upright. If he wasn't going to call the police, at least we could help clean up.

"Oh, you don't have to do that. I'll get things cleaned up in a jiffy," he said as he continued to sweep, filling the dustpan with chips and the bags they had come from. He turned and dumped it into a nearby trashcan. "It won't take me long to get things cleaned up."

"We'll help," Dad said, picking up a large wire rack and setting it upright. "It's bad enough that they steal your cash register and the money in it, but then they've got to destroy things just for the heck of it."

Bill sighed. "Yes, it seems it's adding insult to injury." He sniffed.

"This is awful," Chloe said. "I can't believe somebody is going around town doing something like this."

"People aren't raised right these days," Henrietta said, opening the trash bag she held.

"No one seems to care anymore," Mom agreed, picking up a small display that had held sunblock and had sat on the counter. The robbers had stomped on some of the tubes and sunblock was squirted all over the floor.

"How did they get into the shop?" Dad asked as he picked up another rack.

Bill jerked his head back toward the small back room. "Back door. There's a wall behind the shop there, and that probably did a good job of hiding them from anyone who might notice what they were doing."

Dad shook his head. "That's awful."

Bill looked at Chloe. "I heard they broke into your

mom's shop, and they did more than just steal the cash register. They left a dead body in the walk-in freezer. Is that true?"

Chloe nodded as she picked up bags of chips. "Yes, it's true. We're not sure why the dead guy was there, but we think two people were robbing the shop, and for some reason, one ended up in our walk-in freezer. The other person who was with him had to have jimmied the handle on the inside so it couldn't be opened."

Bill shook his head. "I don't know what gets into people. Robbing, murdering, and just damaging things because they can. I tell you; I don't know what this world is coming to. I've worked hard all my life to support myself and my family, and this is how I'm repaid for it."

Henrietta made a sound of disgust as she picked up smashed sandwiches from the floor and put them in the trash bag.

My heart went out to them both. They were good people and had been friends with our family for years. They didn't deserve to be treated this way.

"Let me call Noah. He needs to know about this." I inhaled, trying to shake off the frustration.

"I don't know. It's been happening all over town. It

won't matter that one more business was hit," Bill said. He was beginning to sound dejected, and while I didn't blame him, it broke my heart. He was always so upbeat whenever we came into the shop.

"Bill, why don't you go ahead and go fishing with my dad?" I suggested. "Chloe, my mom, and I will stay here with Henrietta and clean up the shop."

He turned and looked at me. "Oh, no, I couldn't do that. There's so much to do here."

"It might help you relax," Chloe said. "I know how stressful this kind of thing can be. Believe me, I know it firsthand. We don't mind cleaning up for you."

Bill shook his head and continued sweeping. "No, I appreciate the offer, but I need to clean this place up. I've got a locksmith on the way. They're going to replace the lock on the back door. I'm going to ask him if he's got a stronger lock than what I've got back there." Bill suddenly burst into tears, and I went to him and hugged him. Then my mom and my dad did, too.

"Bill, go ahead and go," Henrietta said softly. "Me and the girls will take care of things."

He looked up at his wife. "I've worked all my life for this business," he finally said. "I don't know how I'm going to get through this." He turned to us. "I had a lot of money in that cash register. Far too much. It was so stupid. I should have taken it to the bank and dropped it off, but I left it there. This has always been a safe place, and I never worried about being robbed."

I took a deep breath. "Noah is going to find whoever did this. It's going to be okay." I didn't know if I believed my own words. I knew Noah would do his best to find the killer and the robbers, but I didn't know if everything was going to be okay for Bill.

I hugged Henrietta. "I'm so sorry." She nodded, forcing herself to smile.

"Insurance will pay for it, won't they?" Dad asked. "You have insurance, right?"

Bill nodded and wiped at his eyes as he pulled away. "Yes, I've got insurance. I'm just overreacting. I'm sorry."

"This is a stressful situation, and there's nothing to be sorry about," I said. "Honestly, Bill, we would be more than happy to help clean up here. The locksmith will be here, and they will fix the back door. It might be good for you to get some fresh air and spend some time with an old friend."

"Go ahead, Bill," Henrietta encouraged. "The girls will help me."

He hesitated and looked at Dad. "I have been missing my old friend."

Dad nodded. "Me too. What do you say we just go fishing for a while? We don't have to stay long if you don't want to, but I think it would be good for you to get away from this place for a bit."

Bill nodded and handed me the broom and dustpan. "Okay then. You talked me into it. Let's grab some bait and some fishing poles."

It only took a few minutes for Bill and my dad to get what they needed, and they left, leaving Chloe, Henrietta, my mom, and me in silence in the small bait and tackle shop.

With Henrietta's permission, I called Noah.

"I can't believe this happened to you both. You're both too nice for this to happen to." Chloe began sorting through the chips on the floor, looking for bags that hadn't been damaged.

I looked at Henrietta. "This just breaks my heart. You and Bill didn't deserve for this to happen to you."

Henrietta smiled sadly. "Bad things don't ask whether you're good or bad before they happen to you. They just happen."

CHAPTER 12

Noah arrived shortly after Bill and my dad left to go fishing. He took a glance around at the chaos we were still cleaning up. "Looks like they made a mess of things."

I nodded. "I can't believe someone came in here and did this. It makes me sick." I introduced him to Henrietta.

"Did they just tear things up, or did they take anything?" Noah asked her.

Henrietta pulled her sweater tight around herself. "The cash register. They picked it up and took it with them."

Noah shook his head in disgust. "How big is this cash register?"

"Oh, it wasn't big. It was old and fairly small. I never would have guessed that they would just pick it up and run with it." She shook her head, lines creasing her face. "There was a lot of money in it. Too much money." The sound of her frail voice clutched at my heart.

Noah hesitated. "How much?"

She licked her bottom lip and then said, "About eight thousand."

Chloe and I gasped. Bill had said there was a lot of money in it, but I couldn't fathom having that much money in the cash register, especially overnight.

Noah shook his head in disbelief. "Why so much?"

Henrietta shrugged. "Bill kept saying he was going to make a deposit at the bank, but he just didn't get around to it. He feels just awful about it. I guess I should have insisted that he take it down there and make a deposit, but he's always done this. Lots of times he only made a deposit once a week. Or even once every two weeks. It was just foolish." Her eyes went to the mess on the floor as she spoke.

Noah gazed at her, unsure of what else to say. "All right, then," he finally said. "Do you have the serial number for the cash register?"

She nodded. "Sure, we still got the manual from when we bought it years ago. Come on back."

She led the way to the tiny back room, and Chloe and I stared at each other.

"That's a lot of money," she finally said.

I nodded and went back to sweeping. "I'm shocked they left that much in the register." I had lowered my voice because I didn't want Henrietta to hear me say it. I felt terrible for her and Bill, but keeping that much money in the register was risky.

A moment later, Noah and Henrietta emerged from the back room. Noah had the manual and was walking around, looking at the store. "What time did you all get here this morning?" he asked.

"We were here at 5:00 AM. Many of the fishermen drop in to pick up some bait, sandwiches, or drinks to take out on their boats." She sniffed, leaning against the counter.

He nodded. "Why didn't you call sooner?" he asked without looking at her.

"Bill just wanted to clean it up and not tell anybody. He's ashamed because he left so much money in that cash register. I told him we couldn't do that. We had to let the police know just in case they ran into that robber. I know he's been hitting other stores around town, and we don't want him to get away with it. If you all can catch him, are there additional charges for him robbing our store too? Whoever it is needs to go to jail for a long time." Her hands tightened on the edge of the counter as she spoke.

Noah nodded as he walked down the aisles. "Yes, there will be charges for each of the stores he's robbed. We're going to do everything in our power to make sure they're caught."

I glanced up at Noah. "Do you have any suspects?"

He shook his head. "No, not yet, but we'll find them. Especially since they're getting braver. I just came from the hair salon, and they were robbed this morning too."

"Really?" Chloe said. "Two businesses in one night?"

Noah nodded as he came to stand by me. "Two in one night. They're going to mess up. They're taking too many risks, robbing two places just hours apart."

"Oh," Henrietta suddenly said. "I can't believe I almost forgot. We've got an old camera system. There's only one camera, but maybe it caught something."

"Let's take a look at it," Noah said with interest.

We followed Henrietta to the back room. There was an old boxy computer monitor on a table back in the corner. Henrietta had to move things that sat in front of it so we could see the screen. Once she got everything moved, she pushed the button on the front, and it came on with a crackle. The thing looked like it was from the late '80s or early '90s.

She reached beneath the table where the keyboard was and started typing on it before the picture became clear, then she quickly opened a program. "I don't even know if the camera works anymore. It was cheap when bought it, and the picture was never very clear."

"Let's hope it works," Noah said.

A picture suddenly sprang to life, and we were staring at a fuzzy black-and-white image of the bait and tackle shop. The camera was pointed to the area just in front of the door. The door itself wasn't visible in the camera's range. She fast-forwarded the video until we saw a dark image dart across the frame. She rewound it a little so we could see what was happening, and first one person dressed in black darted across the screen, and then a second.

"Two," Noah said to himself. "Can you slow it down a little? I'd like to see if I can see their faces."

Henrietta did as he asked, but the camera image was so bad it wouldn't matter how slowly you ran it. It was fuzzy and dark, and I couldn't imagine being able to figure out who these people were.

"It's an awful image, isn't it?" Henrietta said to no one in particular.

"It is," Noah agreed. "Run that second one again."

The image of the second person crossing the camera came up on the monitor again. This person was smaller than the first. "If I'm not mistaken, that looks like a woman," Noah said.

"I agree," I said. "It looks like a woman, just by the way she moves, and that she's smaller than the first person."

"I think it's a woman too," Chloe agreed.

After watching them kick over displays and destroy merchandise in the store, they disappeared off-screen for a while and then returned with the larger person carrying the small cash register. It made me sick to actually watch it happen. The two disappeared, heading toward the door.

Henrietta sighed. "It's even worse having to watch it, even if it isn't a clear picture."

Noah nodded. "I'd like to get a copy of this footage. I don't know if it will really help me find out who did this, but it's good to have it anyway. I know this doesn't help right now, but cameras have gotten rather inexpensive these days. It would be worth it to have an updated system."

Henrietta nodded. "I'll talk to Bill about it. It's just that when you rarely have trouble, you don't stop and think about these things."

"Noah, did the salon have better cameras?" I asked.

He nodded. "They did, but the robbers were hiding their faces. And only one was in the camera's range. There were two there, but the first one stayed out of the camera frame most of the time."

Chloe and I looked at each other. Whoever these people were, we were going to figure out their identity.

CHAPTER 13

After we cleaned up the bait and tackle shop, Chloe and I stopped by the nail salon where Ashley Myers worked. She had been Charlie's girlfriend when he was murdered, so she would know something about what was going on in his life shortly before he died, wouldn't she?

We stepped into the nail salon, and two other customers were being worked on by other nail technicians. When Ashley saw us, she stood up from her table and hurried to the counter. "Good morning, ladies. Did you have an appointment?"

I shook my head. "No, I'm sorry, we don't have an appointment. Do you take walk-ins?" Ashley was petite, no more than 5'4". Could she have killed Charlie as Ryan said? I couldn't see how.

She smiled. "Now and then we can take a walk-in, and it's just your luck that I had a cancellation this morning. Do you know what you want done?"

I smiled. "I think I just want a manicure and a clear coat. I haven't had a manicure in forever, and a clear coat will make my hands look nice."

"I think I'd like the same if you can fit me in, too," Chloe said.

She nodded. "A manicure and a clear coat will take no time at all. I'll have enough time for both of you. Follow me."

We followed her back to her station, and she pulled up an extra chair for Chloe. I sat in the chair behind the table, and she sat across from me. "Don't I know you girls? Don't you work at the ice cream shop?"

We both nodded. "Yes, Cookie's Creamery," Chloe said. "I've seen you around. Your name is Ashley, isn't it?"

She nodded, averting her eyes, and looking a bit pale now. "Yes, Ashley Meyers. Oh, wait a minute, did I do your nails once?" She asked, looking at me.

I nodded. "Yes, it's been about three or four years

ago. You did a nice job on my nails for Christmas one year."

"Ha! I knew I had worked on you before." She smiled triumphantly at having remembered me. She got everything ready for my manicure and then got to work on my hands. She glanced up at me, but didn't say anything more.

"So, Ashley, did you hear about the murder last week?" I asked after a few minutes of silence, keeping an eye on her face for her reaction.

She looked up at me. Her long, curly blond hair was loose, with a thick lock having fallen across her face. "Yeah, there was no way I wasn't going to hear it. Charlie was my boyfriend."

"I'm so sorry," Chloe said.

I nodded, trying not to let on that we already knew this. "You must be devastated. I'm sorry you're going through this. It was so sad that he died the way he did."

She sighed and kept working on my cuticles. "Isn't it though? I tell you; I don't know what has gotten into people these days. It's like they commit crimes and don't even think twice about it. I talked to Charlie's dad the other day, and he said the police still hadn't figured out who killed him. Can you imagine?"

Her eyes met mine. "What is taking the police so long to find his killer?"

I had a sneaking suspicion that she knew I was dating the detective on the case. "I'm sure finding a murderer takes a lot of time. There are clues to put together, and they don't want to make a mistake about anything when they arrest a suspect."

She hesitated and nodded. "Oh, I'm sure. I bet tracking down a killer isn't an easy prospect. Correct me if I'm wrong, but aren't you dating that detective?"

I nodded. "I am dating the detective on the case. And I can tell you firsthand that he is doing everything possible to find whoever killed Charlie."

She nodded without looking at me. "I'm sure he is. I just can't get over that somebody would murder him."

"Had you seen him recently before he died?" I asked.

She glanced at me. "Yeah, I saw him that day. We were making plans for the weekend. I wanted to go out on one of those fishing boats for the afternoon and just hang out. I don't like fishing, but it's fun to go out on the ocean in a boat like that."

"Did Charlie like to fish?" Chloe asked.

She shook her head. "No, fishing is too dirty and

stinky." She laughed. "Charlie didn't like to get dirty. I just can't figure out why he would end up in that freezer at the ice cream shop." She looked at me. "Had he been in the ice cream shop before he died?"

I was taken aback by the question. I felt like she was mirroring the question I had asked her about whether she had seen Charlie right before he died. I shook my head. "I don't remember seeing him come into the ice cream shop. But sometimes we get really busy, and it's hard to remember who we've seen during the day."

"I don't remember seeing him either," Chloe said. "Why? Did he mention he was going to stop in?"

She glanced at Chloe and then shrugged. "I don't know. I can't figure out what he was doing in the ice cream shop and how he ended up in that freezer is all. It's weird, don't you think?"

Chloe nodded. "Oh, yes, it's very weird. You don't have any idea why he would have ended up there?"

She shook her head without looking at either of us while working on my hands. "No, I don't have any idea what he would be doing there." She was quiet for a few moments, then looked up at me. "If I had to take a wild guess, I would say that his brother killed him."

I was surprised to hear this. "Oh? Why would you think that?"

She shrugged. "The two didn't get along that well. They bickered a lot."

I shook my head. "Bickered? Why would that be enough for his brother to have killed him?" I hadn't thought about Ryan being Charlie's killer, mostly because I couldn't see a reason he would do it.

She gazed at me, and there was something behind that gaze that I couldn't quite put my finger on. It was like she thought I was stupid for asking the question. "You don't know Ryan like I know him. But then, how would they have ended up in that ice cream shop?" She shrugged and laughed. "Well, I guess I don't know much, do I? I'm sure the police will figure out who killed Charlie."

I gazed at her, unsure of what to make of all this. "Is there a reason you think Ryan might have killed him?"

She shook her head. "No, I really don't have a good reason. I guess I shouldn't have said anything. I just get tired of waiting for the police to figure out who killed Charlie. Can you talk to your boyfriend and ask him to hurry up and find his killer?"

I wanted to sigh loudly. As if Noah wasn't already doing everything he could to find Charlie's killer. "Sure, I'll pass that along. But I assure you he is doing everything he can to find the murderer." I decided then and there that I did not like Ashley. I could see why Hugh Dade didn't care for her, either.

CHAPTER 14

I looked up when the bell over the door jingled, and Harold Billingsley walked in. He smiled and hurried to the counter. Chloe was still waiting on a customer, but I had just finished with one and was free.

"Good afternoon, Harold. How are you doing?" I asked, wiping my hands with a paper towel.

He smiled and nodded. "I guess I'm doing okay. I got the day off from work, so I can't complain. Looks like I made it right in time; no line."

I chuckled. "You just missed the long line. You've got perfect timing. What can I help you with?"

He scanned the ice cream freezer. "Oh, why don't

you get me a sugar cone with a double scoop of chocolate ice cream and a sugar cookie?"

"You got it." I grabbed a sugar cone and an ice cream scoop.

"I heard you all had a little trouble here last week," he said and leaned on the counter.

I glanced at him as I opened the ice cream freezer. "Yeah, we had a little trouble last week." I decided not to elaborate. Too many people were coming in and asking us about the murder, and I didn't like it.

"Heard Charlie Dade ended up dead in your ice cream freezer. I hope this ice cream wasn't kept back there with him." He tapped on the freezer's glass.

My eyes cut to him. "I assure you, our ice cream is kept under the cleanest conditions, and we pass every health inspection with an A."

He nodded. "Oh, sure, I know you do. Cookie's has got the best ice cream on the planet. And I don't blame anybody for wanting to kill Charlie Dade. He had it coming."

I scooped the first scoop of chocolate ice cream, placing it firmly on the cone. "Oh? Why do you say that?" Some people just like to talk, and I wasn't sure if that's what Harold was doing now or if he knew something.

He nodded again. "He was a liar and a cheat. He sold me a laptop from that electronics store he worked for that was used. The trouble was, he told me it was brand new and charged me that way." He shoved his hands into the pockets of his black pants and jingled his keys. "Well, more specifically, I guess he never actually said it was new, but he didn't say it was refurbished either. But believe me, the price he charged me was for new, so how was I to know any different?"

I glanced at him. "Really? Why would he do something like that? And couldn't you just bring it back and get your money back?"

He shook his head. "No, because it was refurbished, there was only a 90-day warranty on it, and I was just past the warranty by four days when it died on me. Can you believe that? Four days. Charlie knew it was going to do that, too. He wasn't the least bit worried about me bringing it back before then, and when I brought it back, the manager said the warranty was out, and there was nothing he could do about it."

I scooped the second scoop of chocolate ice cream and placed it on top of the first. "Couldn't you tell it was refurbished? Weren't there any nicks or dings on it?"

He shook his head. "No, that thing looked brand new. Clean as a whistle. It worked just great, too, until it passed its warranty. That was when it got really slow, and then it completely crashed."

I grabbed a handful of napkins and handed him the ice cream cone with the napkins. "Well, how could he have known that it was going to last just until the warranty expired? There's no way he could have known something like that."

He shrugged. "I have no idea, but I'm telling you, he knew. That manager should be ashamed of himself for not giving me my money back. I was cheated, and he knew it."

I couldn't get past the fact that the computer looked brand new. There had to be a chip or scratch somewhere, didn't there? "What about the keyboard? Weren't any of the letters or numbers faded? A used keyboard gets that way."

He shook his head again. "No, I'm telling you, the laptop looked brand new. If I had had the slightest hint it was refurbished, I wouldn't have bought it."

"That's a shame," I said, as we headed to the

register so I could ring him up. Then I realized I had forgotten the cookie. "Let me get your cookie."

"What I think he did was, he took some of the better refurbished laptops and sold them as new, pocketing the difference for himself. If the books at the computer store showed he was selling a refurbished one, then he wouldn't have been in trouble with them." He raised his voice so I could still hear him.

I tucked a sugar cookie into a small bag and brought it back to the register, and handed it to him. "I guess I can see how somebody might do something like that." I rang up his ice cream cone.

"I think he did it to the wrong person. I think he sold a lemon of a laptop to somebody who took it personally, and they murdered him. It serves him right, you know. The only way anybody was ever going to stop him was to put an end to him." He dug into his pocket for some money.

I gazed at him. I'd already heard so many theories, and I was tired of hearing them, but what if this was true? "Let's say that happened," I said as I took the money from him. "Why would they have brought him *here* to kill him? That doesn't make any sense to me. They could have killed him anywhere, and there would have been less chance of them being caught. Anybody could have seen them as they were breaking into the ice cream shop."

He paused for a moment. "I guess I don't have an answer to that. But I don't care. Whoever killed Charlie Dade did everyone a favor. In fact, if they hadn't done it, I might have taken care of it. He ripped me off, and he needed to pay."

"Harold, you don't mean that. You shouldn't be saying things like that when his murderer hasn't been found. The police might take a closer look at you if you go around saying that to the wrong person." Harold was in his mid-thirties and didn't strike me as the kind of person who would murder someone, but I'd been wrong before.

He shrugged. "I've got an alibi for that night. I'm safe." He stared at me for a moment, then turned and walked out the door.

Chloe sidled up to me. "I can't believe he just said that," she whispered.

I shook my head. "Me either." Some people didn't have enough sense to shut their mouths.

CHAPTER 15

I looked across the table at Noah as he finished his meal. It felt like it had been forever since we'd gone out to dinner together, and I had been looking forward to it ever since he texted me earlier that morning asking if I was available for dinner. I was. My parents had left before 6:00 a.m., and the house was a little lonely without them, so spending time with Noah this evening was perfect timing.

"What?"

I smiled. "What do you mean, 'what'?"

He chuckled. "Why are you looking at me like that?"

I shook my head. "I'm not looking at you in any particular way. I'm just stuffed and happy."

He grinned and nodded. "I'm pretty stuffed myself. They make the best steaks here. We need to come more often."

"You won't get any complaints from me," I said. "My T-bone was cooked perfectly. Plus, I love the fresh bread they serve here. You can always tell how good a restaurant is by the quality of the bread they serve with their meals."

"I can't argue with you there. The bread was excellent, and I've never had bad bread at a good restaurant." He took a sip of his iced tea and set the glass down. "I hate to say this, but I'm about to fall asleep, and we probably should go soon. I haven't been sleeping well lately."

I shook my head. "Don't worry about it. I know you're tired, and I don't blame you. You work hard on these investigations." I was a little disappointed, but I wasn't going to complain. Solving a murder took intense focus and work.

He gazed at me, then his eyes widened. "Oh. I forgot to tell you. I got some of the reports back for the fingerprints we took at some of the shops that were broken into."

I looked at him with one eyebrow raised. "How could you forget that? What did the report say? Please tell me there's good news that will lead to finding Charlie Dade's killer."

"I don't know if it's going to help find his killer, but it was interesting, nonetheless. We found Charlie's fingerprints at three of the four shops that were broken into before his death."

My eyes widened. "So, he *was* one of the robbers. He must have been double-crossed by his partner, and they shoved him into the freezer at Cookie's." We had been operating under the assumption that he had something to do with the break-ins, but to actually have evidence that he was there was fantastic to hear.

He took another sip of his iced tea. "Right. That must have been the way it went down. So, we have to figure out who his partner was. We have the video that Deborah Carr supplied, and we have the video from Bill and Henrietta's bait shop. But we haven't been able to get any other video from the other shops."

I shook my head. "Why not? Don't most businesses have cameras these days? I even have some at my house now."

He nodded. "I guess in a place like Lilac Bay, people don't feel it's necessary. Or, like Bill and Henrietta, they don't replace them once they have them. And both George Salyard's and Blake Rountree's video cameras were malfunctioning. The battery in Calen Johnston's camera was dead, so we don't have any video from them."

I sighed, debating whether I wanted another piece of bread. Or rather, I debated on whether I could hold another piece because I wanted another one. "So, if that was a female on Bill and Henrietta's video, it has to be Ashley Myers. She and Charlie had a volatile relationship with frequent breakups and then getting back together, and they had recently gotten back together again before Charlie was killed. And she was weird when Chloe and I went to talk to her. She didn't seem at all sad that Charlie was murdered. The other person could have been her brother, Rickey."

"And it's always the weird ones, right?" he said with a wink.

I chuckled. "You know what I'm saying. There was just something about her. For a moment it seemed like she thought she had said too much. But she's petite, and I'm wondering if she really could have shoved him into that freezer."

He nodded. "Plus, she had to disable that handle inside. She would have needed tools and the strength to do it, and I don't know if she has that strength." He picked up his fork and moved it around the remnants of his salad on the plate. "Unless it was somebody else. Or maybe it's not a woman, but a smaller man. But it wasn't Rickey with her."

I looked up at him. "Why isn't it?"

"Because he's been in county lockup for stealing a car since before Charlie was murdered. It's a great alibi."

I sighed. "Okay, it has to be somebody else, then. But the smaller person moves like a woman. Don't you think so?"

He nodded and sighed. "It could be. Let's get out of here." We paid the bill, and left the restaurant. "Oh, I forgot to tell you. I spoke to Harold Billingsley—he bought a refurbished laptop from Charlie who had told him it was new. The hard drive failed, and it was out of warranty, so you can imagine how angry he is about that. He told me it was a good thing someone else killed him or he would have done it himself."

Noah glanced at me. "Do you think he was serious?"

I shrugged. "I don't know. But it's kind of a dumb

thing to say when Charlie's killer hasn't been found yet."

"True. I'll keep it in mind." He wrapped his arm around my waist as we walked. "It's a beautiful night."

"I love the month of June," I said as I squeezed him with one arm. "And I love summer nights."

"Me too."

Across the street from the restaurant was a small park, and we headed over there and sat on the old-fashioned merry-go-round. We squeezed over as close to one another as we could get with the metal bars that came out from the center and then provided a slight barrier to keep kids from flying off of it between us. Rumor had it that the metal poles didn't do a great job keeping kids on the ride.

"Hey."

I turned to look at him. "What?"

He gazed into my eyes. "I love you."

My heart began to pound as I stared breathlessly at him. It was the first time he had told me that he loved me. I would like to have said that I answered him intelligently, but instead, I broke down blubbering.

"Oh, don't do that. Why are you crying?" he asked, pulling me to himself with the bar separating us.

I laid my head on his shoulder and sobbed. It took what felt like forever for me to pull myself together, but when I did, I looked up at him. "I love you, too."

He smiled, and tears came to his eyes. "Thank goodness. I was afraid for a minute there you were going to tell me that you wanted to break up."

"Why would I say something like that?"

He shrugged sheepishly. "Because you just started crying and didn't answer me."

I chuckled and kissed him. "Don't be silly."

He leaned his forehead against mine. "I really do, you know. I love you."

"I love you, too."

We held each other tight for a while. This was one of the happiest days of my life.

CHAPTER 16

The scent of freshly baked bread wafted through the room when Chloe said, "Okay, spill it."

I looked across the table at her. "Spill what?"

"You've practically been shining all morning long. What's going on? You're so happy."

My brow furrowed. "What do you mean, 'I'm so happy'? Aren't I always happy?"

She rolled her eyes. "Of course you're always happy, but this is something more. What's going on?"

I broke out into a grin. I couldn't help myself. "Noah told me he loves me."

Chloe gasped. "Oh, my gosh! That's wonderful! Is it the first time he said it? Wait, of course, it's the first time. You wouldn't be so excited otherwise. Did you tell him you loved him back? *Do* you love him back?"

I laughed. "Of course I said I loved him back, because I do. Oh, my gosh. I can hardly believe that he said it. He loves me. And I love him. Oh, Chloe, I've never been this happy. Never." I took a deep breath to steady my nerves.

"Oh, that's so wonderful," she gushed. "I'm so happy for you, Maddie. When are you getting married?"

I laughed. "Married? Come on, we just love each other and we're happy with that much for right now."

She sighed. "I know, I'm just teasing. I'm so happy for you, Maddie. I'm jealous."

"Chloe, we've got to get you a man. You deserve all the happiness in the world." Chloe frequently went out on dates, but she hadn't found anyone she thought she wanted to be with long-term. She was my best friend, and I wanted to see her happy. We were going to have to find someone for her to go out with.

She shook her head. "It will happen in time. I'm not worried."

I nodded. "It will. Just wait and see."

I turned back to my menu. We were on our lunch

break at a local café, and I was starving. "I think I'm going to get the ham and cheese sandwich with potato salad."

She nodded. "I'm going with the turkey avocado."

The waitress returned, took our orders, and removed the menus.

Chloe took a sip of her lemonade. "So, anything new in the case?"

I shook my head. "I don't think so. I already told you about the fingerprints. How is your mom doing? Every time I ask her how she is, she says 'fine,' but she's quieter than she normally is." I was worried about Cookie, and I hoped that when the killer was found, she would return to being her old self.

She nodded. "Yes, and it worries me. She won't tell me how she's really feeling. She's still so upset about finding Charlie's body in our freezer."

"I don't blame her, but I certainly hope she's gotten past thinking that she's somehow responsible for him ending up there."

She nodded. "I think she is. We talked about that the other day, and she agreed with me when I told her it had nothing to do with her. I think she'll be fine once Noah arrests the killer. I'm pretty sure that's really what's bothering her, and until that happens, she's going to worry."

I took a sip of my iced tea. "I don't blame her. If it had been my shop where somebody was murdered, it would upset me too. But she has no business taking any of the blame on herself."

Cookie had always been the sensitive type, and she was the sweetest person I knew. It didn't surprise me she was taking on too much of a burden where this was concerned.

* * *

We finished with our lunch and paid for our meals. When we got up from the table to leave, I stopped in my tracks.

"What?" Chloe asked. I turned to look at her and then nodded toward the table at the end of the walkway.

She turned, and her eyes widened. Jared Stone and Ashley Myers were sitting at an intimate, out of the way table. Both of them leaned forward over their table in what looked like an intimate conversation.

"What do you suppose that's about?" Chloe whispered.

I shook my head. "I don't know, but let's go see."

We walked the short distance to their table and stopped in front of it. It took them a moment to realize we were there, but when they turned and looked, Ashley's eyes widened, and Jared's mouth dropped open.

"Hi, Ashley, hi Jared. Fancy meeting you two here," I said. "What did you order for lunch? I had the ham and cheese, and it was wonderful. They have the best bread that they make their sandwiches with here."

"I got the turkey and avocado," Chloe said. "I highly recommend it. They put lots of tomatoes on it, and I absolutely love tomatoes."

They both stared at us, trying to gather their wits about them.

"Oh, hey, Maddie, Chloe," Jared finally said. "What a surprise, seeing you two here. What's going on?"

I shook my head. "We were just getting away from the ice cream shop to get a little lunch. How are you doing, Ashley?"

She forced a smile, and nodded. "I'm doing well. I happened to run into Jared outside the café, and we decided there was no reason for us to eat alone, so we got a table together."

I almost groaned. The way those two were leaning toward each other, their eyes locked in conversation, they did not just meet out on the sidewalk. "Oh gosh, talk about timing."

"Yeah, that was perfect timing," Chloe echoed.

Jared nodded. "Yeah, imagine that. We've known each other for a few years now so it's nice to get to catch up and talk about old times."

"Old times?" I asked. "You two used to date?"

"Oh, no, we never dated," Ashley said quickly. "We've just known each other for a long time, that's all." She smiled again.

Jared glanced at Ashley and then turned back to me. "Yeah, we've known each other for a few years. We worked together about five years ago. It was a lot of fun, but we haven't seen each other around town much lately. That's why we wanted to catch up."

I nodded. "Ashley, how are you doing? I know it has to be so hard for you that Charlie's killer hasn't been found yet."

She sobered and nodded. "Yes, it's killing me that the killer hasn't been found. No pun intended. I think I'm going to stop by the police station and talk to Noah again. Did he mention to you if he had anything new on the case?"

I shook my head. "No, he hasn't mentioned anything. But I know he's putting a lot of time into catching the killer. We just have to have patience."

"I'm running out of patience," Ashley said suddenly. "I'll have to stop in and talk to him, like I said."

I nodded. "I think it would be good for you to do that."

We all four looked at each other in silence for a few moments. Ashley was about to say something, but the waitress arrived with their food.

"Well, I guess we'll let you eat in peace," I said. "It was good seeing the two of you." Chloe and I headed out.

"What do you think about that?" Chloe whispered when we got outside.

I shook my head. "It's weird that our victim's girlfriend and the co-worker who couldn't stand him are out to lunch together. Very weird."

They could pretend they had just run into each other in front of the restaurant, but I knew better. And I swore that Ashley had be the smaller of the two people we saw in the videos. She just had to be.

CHAPTER 17

Later, Chloe and I dropped by Lilac Bay Gifts. Charlene Douglas worked there part-time, and I was hoping she would be working today. It was odd that Ashley and Jared were together for lunch since she had been dating Charlie before he died. Maybe I was reading more into it than there was, but it made me wonder. I also wondered whether Charlene had anything interesting to say about her relationship with Charlie or anything else that might help us with the murder.

There was only one other customer in the shop when we walked in, and Charlene was hanging garden flags on a wall with hooks.

"Hey, Charlene," I said as we walked up to her.

She turned to see who had spoken and smiled. "Oh, Maddie and Chloe. How are you girls doing?"

I smiled. "We're doing well. We thought we'd stop in and see what's new in the gift shop. Have you been working here long, Charlene?"

She shrugged. "I guess it's been about eight or nine months now. It's only part-time, but it's a lot of fun. I get to meet lots of people."

"I think it would be a lot of fun working in a gift shop," Chloe said, glancing around at the merchandise. "I think I would probably spend half my paycheck here, though."

Charlene chuckled. "Oh, you have no idea. Every time I tell myself I don't need anything else; we get a new shipment of cute items. These garden flags are so darling. Look at these gnomes. I have a tiny patio at my apartment, and I've got three or four gnomes out there, and these flags would be so cute with them. But I don't need to spend the money."

"I like this one," I said, holding up a flag with a picture of a gnome in front of a lilac bush. It really was cute, although I wasn't into gnomes.

She nodded. "See? They're just too cute."

"Charlene, how are you doing?" I asked gently. I had meant to stop in to see how she was getting on after we had talked to her at the ice cream shop, but things just seemed to get in the way.

A shadow crossed her face, and she frowned. "I can't believe how much I miss Charlie. We planned to get married. I don't know if you knew that or not." She turned away from me and hung up the flag she had in her hand.

"Oh, no," Chloe said. "I'm so sorry. I didn't realize you were going to get married." She shot me a look.

Charlene turned back to us, her eyes glistening with unshed tears. "Yeah, I was crazy about Charlie. He was the nicest guy I've ever dated. We had all kinds of plans for a big wedding, but we didn't have any way to pay for it." She chuckled sadly. "That's why I took this job on top of my other job at the grocery store. I was saving up to help pay for the wedding."

"I'm so sorry," I said. "This has to be so hard."

She nodded without looking at me. "Yes, I was devastated when I found out about Charlie. I can't imagine who would do such a thing to him. But the thing is, we had broken up a couple of months ago." She looked at me now, and I thought she would burst into tears.

My heart went out to Charlene. "If you don't mind me asking, what happened?"

She shook her head. "It was Ashley—that girl is wild, and she threw herself at Charlie. They had dated previously, and maybe he wasn't over her. I don't know. All I know is that I have never had my heart broken as much as when he told me he was getting back together with Ashley." She hung up another flag. "But what was I supposed to do? He wanted to be with her."

"That's awful," Chloe said. "Really, it stinks."

She nodded and opened the flaps of the cardboard box on the cart in front of her to see into it better. "I still can't get over it. My parents were going to contribute a significant amount of money to help pay for the wedding, and I took on this job, and it was just going to be beautiful. I had so many plans." She sighed. "And then he told me it was over."

I felt bad for Charlene, but it seemed like she should have had some indication that something wasn't quite right between the two of them, wouldn't she? "That's terrible."

She turned back to me. "I can't believe he did that to me. But a couple of days before he died, he started texting me. He wasn't happy with Ashley. I think if he hadn't died, we would have gotten back together. He loved me, you know. He could never love Ashley the way he loved me. It's just that Ashley—well, she's trash. She threw herself at him, and it was just—I don't know—a momentary weakness on his part. He would have come back to me. I'm sure of it."

I nodded. "Relationships can be tricky sometimes. Maybe he just needed a little time to think."

"Some guys get weird when faced with their own wedding," Chloe pointed out. "Maybe he just needed time to think, like Maddie said."

She nodded and removed two garden flags from the cardboard box. "I'm sure that's what it was. But now he's gone, and I have to live with this for the rest of my life. I should have gone to him when he started texting me again and told him I wanted to be with him forever. I just know that it would have been enough to make him dump Ashley." She sighed, then looked at me. "I think Ashley saw our texts. She had to be the one who killed him. She was crazy. They would get into fights, and she would hit him. I think they must have argued. Maybe he told her he was leaving her for me, and she became enraged. I just know she's his killer."

I hesitated. Was it true? Did Ashley kill Charlie because she saw their texts? We had just seen her with Jared, and while they tried to behave as if they hadn't planned to have lunch together, neither Chloe nor I believed it. But if we were right, why would she be with Jared so soon after Charlie's death?

"If you have any specific evidence that she may have killed Charlie, then you need to talk to the police," I said.

She held a flag to her chest. "Well, I don't have any specific evidence. But I'm basing it on what I know about Ashley and Charlie. Ashley has a temper, and she would hit him. It's only one more step to kill him."

I was sure it was more than one step to go from hitting somebody to killing them, but I didn't say so. She might have been right about Ashley, though. The more I found out about her, the more I thought she had to be the killer.

CHAPTER 18

"Ambrosia ice cream sounds good," I said, looking up at the whiteboard. We had been at work for almost two hours now and it was almost time to open. The ambrosia ice cream was the last flavor left to make.

"I'll work on that one," Cookie said. "I'm still experimenting with the recipe."

"That recipe is perfect just the way it is," Chloe said as she checked on the maraschino cherry chunk cookies baking in the oven.

Cookie shook her head. "You know how I am. I've got to make sure it's perfect for its debut." She chuckled. "I bet most people don't realize new ice cream flavors need to make a debut."

I smiled. Cookie had been so down since we had discovered Charlie Dade's body in our freezer, and it was nice to see her laugh. "Well, I, for one, am waiting with bated breath for ambrosia ice cream. It sounds delicious."

She looked at me and smiled. "I certainly hope it will be. How are things going on the murder investigation?"

I shrugged. "You know how it is. Noah is working night and day on this case."

"And we've been asking around, trying to figure things out," Chloe said as she grabbed an oven mitt to remove the pan of cookies from the oven.

Cookie eyed us. "I hope you girls will be careful. I'd hate for anything awful to happen to you while you're asking around. I'm sure some people don't appreciate you two looking into the murder. Like, the murderer, for one."

"We try to be careful," I said. I started to say something else, but there was a banging noise on the front door as if somebody were trying to get in.

Cookie's brow furrowed. "Now, who could that be?"

I shook my head, and we went to the kitchen door

to look out. The sound continued, but we didn't have a good view of the front door from here.

"Let's be careful, girls," Cookie said as we slowly made our way out front. When we had a good view of the glass front door, Cookie said, "Oh, it's Deborah Carr."

Deborah had a look of terror on her face as she pulled on the door handle. I hurried over and unlocked the door. "Deborah, what's going on?"

She pulled her cardigan tightly around herself, and I stepped back to allow her inside, locking the door behind her. "Oh my gosh, you girls won't believe what happened. Somebody broke into my gift shop."

"Oh, no," Chloe said.

"That's terrible," Cookie echoed.

She nodded. "I just can't believe it. They destroyed merchandise in my shop, knocking things over, and then they broke into the cash register and stole the money in there. Why, I didn't even have that much in there—not more than a hundred dollars."

"Did you call the police?" I asked.

She nodded. "Yes, Noah just left a few minutes ago. I just can't believe this. What is this town coming to? Why are all these shops getting broken into?"

Lines creased her forehead, and she looked like she was ready to cry.

"It seems somebody is determined to ruin the businesses here in Lilac Bay," Cookie said, frowning.

I hugged Deborah. "I'm so sorry. This is just awful."

She nodded, and tears came to her eyes. "It is terrible. Why even bother robbing the shops when most of us don't keep very much money in there overnight? I know they stole a few things from my shop, but when you think about it, it wasn't worth enough money to put themselves at risk like that."

When she said that, I thought about Bill and Henrietta. They had lost far more than a hundred dollars from their cash register, and it still made me sick to think about it. The robbers may have been hoping there were more businesses that kept large amounts of money in their cash registers.

There was another knock at the door, and I turned to look. Estelle was standing there, smiling at me through the glass. I glanced at the clock; it was three minutes after. I hurried over and unlocked it, and let her in. "Good morning, Estelle. It's so nice to see you."

She stepped inside the ice cream shop. "I hope

I'm not disturbing anything. I was out on my walk, and you know how I am. I've got to have my ice cream."

"You're not interrupting anything," I said. "Let's go look at the ice cream and see what you would like."

"Certainly," she said, but she hesitated when she saw Deborah. "Good morning, Deborah. How are you this morning?"

Deborah shook her head. "Not well, I'm afraid. My gift shop was broken into overnight. I still can't believe it."

Estelle gasped. "Oh, how awful. Did they get very much? Is everyone okay? I hope no one was hurt."

She shook her head. "No one was there; it happened around three o'clock in the morning. They didn't get a lot of cash, only about a hundred dollars. I think they stole a few things, but otherwise, they just made a mess, knocking displays over and breaking things."

"That's just terrible," Estelle said. "I hate to hear that happened to you. I'm so sorry."

"Deborah, how do you know they came in at about 3:00 a.m.?" Cookie asked.

"Oh, I have security cameras. That was the time,

according to the cameras." She sighed. "I hate thieves. It makes me feel so unsafe in my own shop."

"That's great news that they were caught on camera," Chloe said. "Did you get a good shot of their faces? How many were there?"

"There were only two of them, but I didn't get a shot of their faces. They were wearing ski masks. I showed the video to Noah. One of them tripped and fell over one of the displays that the other one had knocked over. Served him right. They had no business being in my shop." Deborah frowned.

"Did it look like he hurt himself badly when he fell?" I asked.

Deborah's brow furrowed. "Well, he had a little difficulty getting back to his feet, and he appeared to be limping after that, but no, I don't think it was a serious injury. I wish it had been. Then if they had to go to the hospital, we might catch them that way."

I nodded. "It's a shame they were wearing ski masks. I know Noah is doing all that he can to find the thieves. I just wish there was a break in this case."

Estelle nodded. "We certainly need a break in this case. I just hate that some thief is running around town, stealing from all the business owners. And then, of course, there was that murder. It worries me that the killer is still on the loose."

"Me too," Deborah said. "I would hate to have come into my store and found a dead body there, as you all did. It's just awful."

Estelle made a clucking sound. "It's just awful."

I moved back behind the counter when more customers entered the shop, and Estelle went to the counter to pick out her ice cream. I felt badly that there was yet another break-in, and I hoped there would be a break in the case soon.

CHAPTER 19

I held Noah's hand as we walked down the Embarcadero. Many of the cute, seaside shops were along this street. We stopped at the surfboard shop, and peered in through the window. They had surfboards, boogie boards, and an assortment of clothing and hats.

"Have you ever surfed?" Noah asked.

I shook my head. "No, it's never really appealed to me. When I was a kid, I always thought you had to have some sort of special ability to balance on the board, and I was quite certain that I did not have that ability. I was sure that I would fall right off and somehow plummet to the floor of the sea."

He looked at me, one eyebrow raised. "Plummet? In water?"

I shrugged. "I was a little kid. I didn't understand that you can't plummet through water unless you have an extremely heavy weight tied to you."

He chuckled. "That would do it."

We moved on to the seashell shop and stopped to look in. "I always wanted to open a seashell shop."

"Maddie sells seashells at the seashore?"

I nodded and grinned. "Yeah. I figured it would be a lot of fun. I also thought that the owner of the seashell shop went out early in the morning every day and searched the beach for seashells. Again, I was a little kid, and hunting seashells was one of my favorite things to do. It never occurred to me I never found enough seashells on any given hunt to stock a shop with."

He chuckled again. "But it would have been fun to see you try to find enough."

We passed restaurants, a bar and grill, and other quaint shops as we walked. The sun wouldn't set for another hour and a half at least, and we were enjoying just hanging out and walking together on a beautiful summer evening.

"I want to stop in at the candy shop up ahead," I said. "I haven't had saltwater taffy in forever."

"I love saltwater taffy. Especially the popcorn flavor."

I grinned. "My favorite is piña colada. The coconut and pineapple always remind me of the tropics."

"Well, we've got to get you some piña colada flavored saltwater taffy then," he said.

"And maybe some chocolate." The Little Seashore Candy Shop sold huge chocolate candies, and I hadn't had one of those in a while, either. Raspberry, chocolate, mint, caramel, and nuts filled each handmade chocolate, and they were the best candies in town. I turned to him. "We need to walk along the Embarcadero more often."

He nodded. "We really should."

The smell of chocolate hung in the air inside the candy shop and made me smile. There was something about the smell of a candy shop that always made me happy. The place was packed so that we had to turn sideways to get by people as we wandered around looking to see what they had. There was crystal rock candy on a display, along with what must have been thirty flavors of saltwater taffy, lollipops, cotton candy, and any kind of chocolate candy you could want. "Can you imagine working in a place like this?"

He nodded. "I'd have a mouthful of cavities if I did, and I'd be twenty pounds heavier."

I chuckled. "Not necessarily. I haven't gained any weight since I started working at the ice cream shop, and you know that's a miracle of sorts." We only used the freshest ingredients at Cookie's, and the ice cream was the best I'd ever eaten, so it was amazing I hadn't made myself sick trying out all the flavors.

We moved in between groups of customers as they excitedly decided on what they were going to buy, and we managed to run straight into Ryan Dade and Charlene. We all stopped just before colliding, and if I had to guess, I would say that the two of them looked shocked to see us. I was pretty sure we had similar looks on our faces.

"Oh, hey, how are you two this evening?" Ryan asked as his eyes darted from me to Noah and back.

Noah nodded. "We're good. How are the two of you?"

I looked at Charlene, who seemed pale this evening. What on earth was she doing with Ryan?

"We're doing great," he said, glancing away.

"Charlene, how are you?" Noah asked.

She looked at him, but she appeared distinctly uncomfortable as she shifted back on her heels. After a moment, she smiled, but that smile didn't reach her eyes. "Oh, I'm great, Detective Grayson. Hi Maddie. What are you two up to?"

"We went for a walk after dinner, and we decided we needed to stop in and get some candy," I said. "What are you two up to?"

She shook her head, still looking uncomfortable. "Oh, we just happened to run into each other outside of the candy shop and ducked inside to see what they had. It's so crowded in here that it's hard to get around, though. I keep running into people." She smiled more genuinely now, and I was pretty sure it was because she thought we were going to buy the story that they just happened to run into each other outside. She wasn't the first person to use that excuse, and I was certain she wasn't telling the truth about it, either.

"It is packed in here," Noah agreed. "What kind of candy are you going to get?"

She shook her head while Ryan looked away. "Oh, we haven't made up our minds. Everything in here looks and smells so wonderful. The chocolate is making me absolutely crazy. I'll have to get something that has chocolate in it."

Ryan turned to Noah. "So, how's the investigation going? Did you find my brother's killer?"

Noah eyed him for a moment before answering. "I'm working on something. I'm hoping to have some answers soon."

If I wasn't mistaken, Ryan turned a shade paler. Why would he be surprised that Noah was about to have some answers soon?

His mouth made a straight line. "Good. I'm glad to hear it. It will give me and my dad some peace, knowing who killed my brother. I wish this wasn't taking as long as it is, because we need those answers."

Noah nodded. "I understand. I wish I could make things move along a little quicker, but we're doing all we can."

Ryan nodded. "Well, I better get some candy picked out. I've got some things to take care of at the house." He glanced at Charlene.

She smiled. "Yes, I've got laundry to do before I go to work in the morning, so I had better get going, too. I'm going to stop at the counter and pick something out of the display case. It was good seeing the two of you." She stepped around us without making eye contact, and headed to the front counter while Ryan headed out the door without getting any candy.

When they were out of earshot, Noah turned to look at me. "That was a surprise."

I nodded. "It certainly was, but I'm pretty sure they did not run into each other in front of the shop. Why does everybody keep saying things like that?"

He shook his head. "I don't know, and I don't know what the two of them would be doing together."

I didn't like this. I didn't like this one bit.

CHAPTER 20

The crush of people inside the candy shop became too much for me, so I let Noah go up to the counter to buy our saltwater taffy and use his good judgment in picking out some chocolates for us. Meanwhile, I sidled out of the shop, weaving between the other customers until I was able to step out into the night air. Although the sun was still up, there was a cool breeze, and I inhaled deeply before exhaling. Crowds made me feel a little like I was suffocating.

I stepped away from the front door so I wouldn't block foot traffic and leaned against a flagpole. That was when I realized that Ryan and Charlene were standing less than five feet away from me. How had

Ryan gotten out of the candy store before I did? They had their backs to me, and their heads were tilted together as they spoke. Curious, I edged a little closer to see if I could hear what they were saying.

People stepped around me as they moved to get in or out of the candy store, and I strained my ears to hear over the din of the crowd, but whatever they were saying, it wasn't loud enough.

I stepped closer and leaned in, hoping I didn't look too obvious, and no one alerted them to my eavesdropping. But the two of them just kept talking, and after a moment, Ryan put his hand on Charlene's lower back at her waist. That seemed intimate. I thought she was so in love with Charlie?

Suddenly, the two stepped forward, and that was when I noticed Ryan had a limp. I hadn't noticed it inside the packed candy store because moving quickly wasn't going to happen in there. He wrapped his arm around her waist more securely, and she leaned into him. For two people who just happened to run into each other outside of the candy store, they seemed awfully cozy with one another.

I increased my pace to keep up with them and glanced over my shoulder, hoping Noah was about finished inside the candy shop, or we were going to get separated. I turned my head to look back. It would be fine. We both had our phones, and I could call him to let him know where I was. But I couldn't let these two get away from me.

"It's fine," I heard Ryan say, the words drifting over the sound of the surrounding people.

What was fine?

They picked up their pace a bit, which exaggerated Ryan's limp. What had happened to him? Had he taken a spill? And that was when I remembered Deborah Carr saying that one of the burglars had tripped and fallen over a display. I quickened my pace a bit so that I was walking very close behind them. The crowd was so thick they didn't seem to notice.

"I don't know," Charlene said. "I'm worried about it."

Ryan shook his head and pulled her closer. "It's fine. Don't let your imagination run away with you. I'll handle everything."

I hurried along behind them, straining my ears to listen, but I couldn't pick up much of what they were saying.

If only they had continued walking quickly, I

wouldn't have bumped into their backs. When I did, Charlene cried out.

"Oh," I said, trying to regain my balance. "I'm so sorry. I wasn't paying attention. Oh, hi Charlene. Hi Ryan." I glanced down at Ryan's leg. "Ryan, what happened to your leg? You're limping."

He frowned. "I took a fall the other day and cracked my knee on the concrete. Why were you following so close?"

I shook my head. "I wasn't following close. At least, I didn't mean to. I was just following behind you, and I wasn't paying attention. I didn't even realize it was the two of you I was following. Sorry." I looked at his knee again. It seemed to be wrapped underneath his jeans.

He stared at me. "You need to watch where you're going."

"Yeah, I will," I said, staring at his knee. "Sorry. Did you see a doctor about your knee? You can really mess up the joint if you aren't careful."

His brow furrowed. "Why are you looking at me that way?"

I looked him in the eye. "What way?"

"You're staring at my knee. Why is it of interest to you?"

I shrugged. "I don't know. You tell me. How did you fall?"

"It was just a little fall," Charlene said. "Nothing serious."

Ryan smiled, but it wasn't a friendly smile. "I guess I wasn't paying attention to what I was doing. Like Charlene said, it was nothing serious."

"Clearly," I said. "I don't suppose you fell over a fixture in the gift shop?"

His eyes widened, and Charlene gasped. "What are you talking about?" Charlene asked. "What display? What gift shop?"

I shook my head. "I think you know the answer to those questions, don't you?"

She shook her head. "I don't know what you're talking about. He did this at his father's house."

"So, his father will vouch for him?" I asked, knowing full well they were lying.

"Of course my father will vouch for me," Ryan said. "That's what fathers do. They vouch for their sons." He smiled slowly.

"I bet they don't vouch for their sons who kill their other sons," I said.

His face turned red. "You better shut your mouth. You don't know what you're talking about. I didn't do anything to my brother. If your boyfriend would get to work and find his killer, my brother could rest in peace."

"He is working on it, and he is going to arrest Charlie's killer so he can rest in peace," I said confidently.

Noah came up behind me and looked from me to them and back again. "What's going on?"

I didn't even bother looking at him. "Ryan seems to have a problem with his knee. He injured it by taking a fall. He claims he did it at his father's house, but if I had to take a wild guess, I would say it happened at the gift shop."

Noah glanced at Ryan's leg again.

"She's crazy," Ryan insisted, pushing hair from his face. "You need to talk to her. She doesn't know what she's talking about."

"It's like she wants to blame Ryan for Charlie's death," Charlene said, narrowing her eyes at me. "And that's the craziest thing I've ever heard."

"Is it?" Noah asked. He held a small white bag with our candy in it and handed it to me. "How did you hurt your knee?" Noah asked.

Ryan chuckled, shaking his head. "Like I said, I fell

at my dad's house. Is it against the law to fall at your dad's house?"

"I'd like to speak with you," Noah said. "Why don't we go someplace quiet to talk?"

Ryan swallowed and then turned and did his best to sprint away. It didn't take much for Noah to catch him, while Charlene ran off in another direction.

CHAPTER 21

Oliver sat on my lap as I watched an old episode of *I Love Lucy*. It was late, but I was still hoping I would get to see Noah. I opened the little white paper bag from the candy store and pulled out a piña colada taffy, unwrapping it slowly. Oliver opened one eye and looked at me sleepily. "You don't like taffy. We've been over this," I said. I popped the taffy into my mouth and savored the sweet flavors. There is nothing like saltwater taffy made at a candy store on the beach during the summer.

A few moments later, there was a knock at my front door, and I jumped, scaring Oliver. I put him down carefully and hurried to the door, peeking through the peephole before opening it.

"Hey," Noah said when I opened the door.

I smiled. "Hey to you, too." I stepped back, and he stepped inside the house, closing the door behind himself.

"I wondered if you would be awake or if I should just go home."

"You know me. I was waiting up." I went up on tiptoes and kissed him. "Tell me what happened."

We went back into the living room and sat down on the couch. I offered him the little white bag. "I've been thinking about this candy. I got myself the buttered popcorn taffy and some salted caramel chocolates. I got you the chocolate-covered cherries."

"I was waiting for you before I ate them."

He nodded, inhaling deeply the scent of the candy wafting out of the bag when he opened it. "Ryan killed his brother. And Charlene helped."

I shook my head. "I was afraid of that. Honestly, I was hoping it was Ashley and not Charlene. Why would she do that? She said she loved Charlie and was saving up for a big wedding with him."

He nodded and grabbed one of the buttered popcorn taffies from the bag, unwrapping it. "She says she loves him, but she was angry because he dumped her and went back to Ashley. As we knew,

Charlie and Ashley had a volatile relationship. Ryan said Charlie had never gotten over Ashley, and every time she wanted back into his life, he never hesitated to take her back. If he was seeing somebody else, he would dump them."

I shook my head. "Wow. That's sad, isn't it? Was Ashley really beating up on Charlie?"

He nodded. "According to Ryan, she was. That's probably where he got that bruise on his side."

"So why did they kill him at the ice cream shop? Why break in and leave him in the freezer?" I still couldn't make sense of that.

He bit the taffy in half, chewed it, and then swallowed before answering. "Charlie and Charlene began the robberies before Ashley came back into the picture. They started robbing businesses, hoping to make enough money to pay for the wedding Charlene wanted. Then Charlie recruited Ryan to help him, and Ryan decided he enjoyed breaking into the shops."

"Figures," I snorted. "He should have taken up a hobby."

"So, when Ashley came back into the picture and Charlie dumped Charlene, he didn't want to do any more robberies. But Charlene knew he had been sneaking around with Ashley before he broke up with her, and she was angry. She got together with Ryan and told him she would help him break into the shops, and they would keep the money for themselves. It was her way of getting back at Charlie."

"Because she still wanted that big wedding, even if it was to marry Ryan?" I asked, as this part of the puzzle clicked.

He nodded. "Yes, she was determined to have that big wedding, even if she wasn't going to marry Charlie. But she and Ryan decided to keep their relationship quiet for the time being." He popped the other half of the taffy into his mouth and chewed. "So good."

I nodded. "It's the best. But why kill Charlie? She had Ryan now."

He shrugged. "Revenge. It wasn't enough for her to have someone else in her life, she wanted revenge. Ryan went along with it because he and Charlie got onto an argument over the robberies. Charlie wanted them to stop because he was afraid we were on their trail and he didn't want to go to jail. Of course, we really didn't know who was committing the robberies."

I shook my head. "Why was Charlie with them

when they broke into the ice cream shop if he wasn't committing any more robberies, then?"

"Charlie and Ashley had a big fight. She got physical with him again, and then he and Ryan argued. Ryan was making fun of him for allowing a woman to beat him up. Charlie's ego couldn't take that, so he threatened to turn Ryan in to the police for robbing businesses. Ryan got scared and thought he would really do it, so he made nice with him and then lured him to the ice cream shop, telling him it would be their last robbery and that he needed his help. Once there, Ryan broke the handle on the inside of the freezer, and they shoved him inside. It was a nice, clean murder where Ryan didn't have to look his brother in the eye while he killed him."

I shook my head. "How horrible. How could they leave him in there, knowing what he was going to go through before he died? I just don't understand it. They were brothers."

He looked into the white paper bag. "You would think being brothers would count for something, but it didn't. Charlene finally realized that Charlie would never come back to her, and she wasn't going to let him get away with cheating and dumping her."

I sighed. "And Ryan and Charlene were just going

to continue breaking into shops, and living as if they weren't murderers?"

He nodded. "They felt it was easy money, and because nobody was there at the shops in the middle of the night, it was less risk to them." He dug into the white paper bag and pulled out one of his chocolates. "Doesn't that look delicious?"

I nodded. "It does look good." I reached over and dug into the bag, and took a chocolate covered cherry out. It smelled heavenly. "I still can't get over the fact that they killed him. Poor Hugh has to live with this for the rest of his life." That was what bothered me most. Hugh Dade seemed like a nice guy, and now he had to find out that his oldest son was murdered by his youngest. I couldn't imagine going through that.

Noah nodded and laid his head on my shoulder. "It's one great big mess. I feel bad for everyone involved, especially Hugh." He dug into the bag and pulled out another chocolate.

Then I remembered something. "What did the key in Charlie's pocket belong to?"

He shrugged. "No one knows. It could have belonged to one of Ryan's bicycles." He yawned. "I'm exhausted. And I really need this chocolate."

I ran my hand through his hair. "I don't blame you for being so tired. Eat your chocolate."

Oliver jumped up on the couch and rubbed up against Noah. He reached out absently and rubbed Oliver's shoulders, then took a big bite of his chocolate.

I leaned back and closed my eyes. This was a sad ending to an even sadder case. The only positive was that Charlie Dade's killers were in jail. Lilac Bay could rest easy.

The End

Sign up to receive my newsletter for updates on new releases and sales:

https://www.subscribepage.com/kathleen-suzette

Follow me on Facebook:

https://www.facebook.com/Kathleen-Suzette-Kate-Bell-authors-759206390932120

BOOKS BY KATHLEEN SUZETTE:

A PUMPKIN HOLLOW CANDY
STORE MYSTERY

Treats, Tricks, and Trespassing
Gumdrops, Ghosts, and Graveyards
Confections, Clues, and Chocolate

A FRESHLY BAKED COZY MYSTERY SERIES

Apple Pie a la Murder
Trick or Treat and Murder
Thankfully Dead
Candy Cane Killer
Ice Cold Murder
Love is Murder
Strawberry Surprise Killer
Plum Dead
Red, White, and Blue Murder
Mummy Pie Murder
Wedding Bell Blunders
In a Jam
Tarts and Terror
Fall for Murder

A FRESHLY BAKED COZY MYSTERY SERIES

Web of Deceit
Silenced Santa
New Year, New Murder
Murder Supreme
Peach of a Murder
Sweet Tea and Terror
Die for Pie
Gnome for Halloween
Christmas Cake Caper
Valentine Villainy
Cupcakes and Beaches
Cinnamon Roll Secrets
Pumpkin Pie Peril
Dipped in Murder
A Pinch of Homicide
Layered Lies

A COOKIE'S CREAMERY MYSTERY

Ice Cream, You Scream
Murder with a Cherry on top
Murderous 4th of July
Murder at the Shore
Merry Murder
A Scoop of Trouble
Lethal Lemon Sherbet
Berry Deadly Delight
Chilled to the Cone
Sundae Suspects
Stars, Stripes, and Secrets

A LEMON CREEK MYSTERY

Murder at the Ranch
The Art of Murder
Body on the Boat

A Pumpkin Hollow Mystery Series

Candy Coated Murder
Murderously Sweet
Chocolate Covered Murder
Death and Sweets
Sugared Demise
Confectionately Dead
Hard Candy and a Killer
Candy Kisses and a Killer

Terminal Taffy
Fudgy Fatality
Truffled Murder
Caramel Murder
Peppermint Fudge Killer
Chocolate Heart Killer
Strawberry Creams and Death
Pumpkin Spice Lies
Sweetly Dead
Deadly Valentine
Death and a Peppermint Patty
Sugar, Spice, and Murder
Candy Crushed
Trick or Treat
Frightfully Dead
Candied Murder
Christmas Calamity

A RAINEY DAYE COZY MYSTERY SERIES

Clam Chowder and a Murder
A Short Stack and a Murder
Cherry Pie and a Murder
Barbecue and a Murder
Birthday Cake and a Murder
Hot Cider and a Murder
Roast Turkey and a Murder
Gingerbread and a Murder
Fish Fry and a Murder
Cupcakes and a Murder
Lemon Pie and a Murder
Pasta and a Murder
Chocolate Cake and a Murder

A RAINEY DAYE COZY MYSTERY SERIES

Pumpkin Spice Donuts and a Murder
Christmas Cookies and a Murder
Lollipops and a Murder
Picnic and a Murder
Wedding Cake and a Murder

Printed in Great Britain
by Amazon